Ask Delilah...
About Cyberlove

A Guide to Computer
Communication

Ask Delilah...
About Cyberlove

A Guide to Computer Communication

AskDelilah@aol.com
a.k.a. Deanna Warren

TIMES ⓣ BOOKS

RANDOM HOUSE

All rights reserved under International and Pan-American Copyright Conventions. Published in the United States by Times Books, a division of Random House, Inc., New York, and simultaneously in Canada by Random House of Canada, Limited.

Grateful acknowledgement is made to the following for permission to reprint previously published material:

Harlequin Enterprises Limited: Excerpt from *Satan Took a Bride* by Violet Winspear. Copyright © 1975 by Violet Winspear. Reprinted by permission of Harlequin Books S.A., Switzerland. Harlequin® is a registered trademark of Harlequin Enterprises Limited.

Ziff-Davis Publishing Company L.P.: 13 symptoms of computer addiction from "How Do You Know When You're Hooked" from *Computer Life* (March, 1995). Copyright © 1995 by Ziff-Davis Publishing Company L.P. Reprinted by permission.

Interior book design by Lynn Rogan
Page composition by Linda Muriello Desktop Typesetting and Publishing Services

ISBN 0-8129-6380-6

Printed in the United States of America on acid-free paper

0 9 8 7 6 5 4 3 2 1

First Edition

He shows up when I least expect it.

He loves to surprise me.

He whispers in my ear, obscene, erotic things that make me feel funny–a dry mouth, a weakness, something low and demanding deep in my gut.

He sticks his tongue into my mouth, tasting my teeth.

He is big, warm, and smells good, of soap and maleness.

He pushes other thoughts away, fills the door of my heart with his presence.

He encourages me to be wholly female, very sexy, and aware of my secret desires.

He encourages me to love him.

He wants my soul.

He is always there, even when quiet.

He wants me to touch myself and know that I am desiring.

He laughs at me and with me.

He makes me *FEEL* in every way.

He lives in my mind.

Delilah

Contents

Contents

Contents

Introduction

::::promising you a wild ride:::

The chief of police in a large midwestern city parked his cruiser beside the highway and waited. He was nervous and excited as he watched the cars rush past. It wasn't his usual duty to sit out on US Route 75, but this frosty morning he waited for a special car, a white Lexus with the Illinois license plate *Sweet1*. His heart jumped when she whizzed by, going at least 10 miles over the speed limit. He had only a second to glimpse the blonde hair, but he could imagine her blue eyes behind the large sunglasses. Flipping on his flare lights, he moved into traffic and was quickly beside her. She looked over at him in surprise, and when he motioned her to pull off the road, a small smile played on her lips. They'd met 3 months earlier on their computers, had seen only pictures of each other, but through hours of conversation had fallen wildly in love. Her real name is Judy and his real name is Tom, and this is a true story.

Tom parked his cruiser behind her car and quickly jumped out. "You said you'd wait for me at the rest stop down the road," she laughed, as he leaned through her window to kiss her warm lips.

"I wanted to get a look at you first," he said. "And anyway, you were speeding, so now I have to arrest you." She looked up at his 6'6" muscular frame, his blond hair and beautiful smile, and her heart did a dance. They spent the weekend together and found each other to be more than they could have hoped for. And Delilah is happy to report that they plan to marry and promise to invite her to their upcoming wedding!

Tom and Judy are not the only ones to have found love on their computers. It is happening every minute all over the world. But whether you're looking for love or just interested in exploring something new, your computer is the genie with the magic. Millions of people have found this to be a wonderful way of sharing information, having fun, and meeting others.

This book is written for the newly curious as well as for the truly addicted onliners, those of us who get up early and stay up late chatting on our computers to people we will probably never meet but know so very well. You know who you are—you are married or not, lonely or not, but you want to be where the action is. You want to understand what all the fuss is about. You enjoy new technology and want an adventure or a bit of excitement. You like to "connect" with a name on your screen, share an intimate thought or story, and take a time-out from your-day-to-day real-life existence.

We will consider the psychology of all this, ask the question "Why is this type of communication so appealing?" and explore some answers. Often quoted Canadian media guru Marshall McLuhan predicted 30 years ago that the world would become a sort of "global village," linking people directly and bypassing traditional boundaries of nations and established cultural values. And we are on our way to that village. The lights are bright and colorful. We can see the pictures and hear the laughter.

We will begin this journey with a glance at the road map and end with a stop on the Internet. Delilah's Internet 101 class will make the "Net" easy to understand, and she shares her favorite 20 Internet newsgroups and 20 World Wide Web sites. We will learn about E-mail and cybersex, that amazing new phenomenon attracting millions to bulletin board services all over the world. And we will peek in our dictionary at the clever language used online. Special abbreviations and symbols add emotion and color to chat and postings, and we will show you how to use these effectively. GMTA means "great minds think alike" and the little smilie on its side, :), can indicate humor when body language is missing and the laughter is behind your screen.

What is cybersex, and who is doing what to whom? Incredible as it sounds, millions of computer users are finding this to be an exhilarating activity, certainly entertaining and often surprising. What fun it is to share an intimate fantasy or cybersex with someone new and exciting. TinyTim, an avid onliner, says, "It is like taking a shower with a raincoat on!" But, hey, even that might be interesting. We will look at what exactly cybersex is and how it works. Is it cheating on your real-life spouse or merely flirting? Those participating say that it depends on your attitude.

Online, age doesn't matter and neither does what we look like or sound like. A 60-year-old woman can enjoy spending time online with a 30-year-old man. It doesn't matter if we are rich or poor. What matters is what we think and how we use words. There are rules and etiquette and even cybercops. A mistake might ruin a friendship forever. And a carefully turned phrase can cement a bond lasting for years. In cyberspace, thoughts and words become more important than physical characteristics, so we will look at how best to express yourself. There are ways of chatting online that get results from others, tried and true methods of getting the attention you hope for.

A deluge of information is available through bulletin boards and the Internet. You can read newspapers and magazines or browse the Library of Congress and the Smithsonian Institute. Your friends online will often be the best source for finding a special newsgroup or visit-

ing an exciting new home page on the Web. In fact, all
this may be so entertaining that you find yourself spending your entire life online. A kind of addiction to this
crazy and wonderful new world is emerging. Delilah will
share her 12-step program to keep this addiction in perspective and under control. Sarah, who enjoys talking
online late at night, says her one-step program works
well for her: "Turn the computer off!"

We will consider how anonymity and distance affect
computer communication. Some online services allow
you to choose a screen name that is different from your
own. You can talk to others through a cloak (or
bathrobe) of anonymity, such as "Dreamdate," and even
make up an imaginary history or profile. Keeping your
identity a secret allows you to be more open and outspoken than you might normally be. Gays and lesbians can
explore the alternative newsgroups and chat rooms
online in a more open atmosphere. And those who wish
can find ample opportunity to experience mind domination and submission in online D/s games, complete with
wild photos and the sound of a whip cracking. "Not all
dominatrixs wear black leather!" insists T.S. on America
Online.

As in most cutting-edge activities, there can be surprises, even dangers. And we would be remiss not to
think about some of these. We will look at the real problem of online stalkers, people who persist in following
another all over cyberspace, stuffing the mailbox full of
unwanted, tasteless missives, using the disguise of
changing screen names and personas, even showing up
on the doorstep! Sometimes even when we think we
know someone well from hours of online conversation,
we can be astonished. Everyone has heard the story of
the eager suitor who flew to another city to meet his
computer love, only to find that she was not the beautiful
lady he imagined but another man! There are ways to

protect yourself online, and we will discuss these.

Just as in real life, men differ from women in the way they communicate online. Men like to discuss their modem speeds and CD-ROM drives. Women like to share stories or poems. But both men and women enjoy making a new friend. Women are, in fact, welcomed online, and more are logging on every day. There are bulletin boards and forums for serious discussions of women's issues. When the women aren't chatting, posting, and E-mailing, where are they? At the mall, of course. Online shopping is becoming increasingly popular. And after a hard day with the kids or at the office, what woman wouldn't love a relaxing warm oil massage—online—carefully described in exquisite detail by her computer mindmate? *Whewwww!*

Can true love also happen? It can and does, every day, just as it did for Tom and Judy. Delilah has heard many more stories from people who have met online, explored personalities, shared pictures and phone conversations, decided to meet, and fallen in love all over again in real life. It is truly a safer place to meet than the local bar or singles' club, and there are so many more possibilities. Think of cyberspace as an interactive personals column. Delilah will share her 10-step plan to finding real-life love. It has worked!

Delilah and millions of others believe that the good things in online socializing far outweigh the bad. There is nothing like being in a room of lively, creative people from all over the world happily sharing a story or game of "Where were you when...?" PeterBB insists his online lady friend has taught him that there is much more to a woman than her sex appeal. "I have learned to appreciate a woman for the total person, what she thinks and feels. Sexual interest can take a secondary role."

In the online world, is there a difference between love and lust? Is it a case of putting the cart before the horse?

Perhaps. But the anonymity of online conversation allows us to explore our emotions and desires in a way that society does not. People feel very open online. They look for friendship and sometimes find love. They are honest, for the most part, and helpful to others. Sharing is a part of this new world. Business contacts are made, jobs are found, the ill get advice and support. Writers find an eager audience for their poetry, stories, and jokes. You can log on anytime day or night to find a home cure for everything from a broken heart to a broken little toe. John S. in Illinois even found help from fellow onliners for the injured goose he found in his backyard. There is a genuine interest in others that is not often found in any other forum.

Psychologists are now using this medium for group therapy. Good therapy is supposed to help you express yourself more fully. It should give you more awareness of feelings about your life. Therapists say they can help you feel better about yourself and be more effective in your work and relationships. And if all of this can be accomplished online, doesn't it follow that you might even be able to overcome the negative effects of past difficulties as well as symptoms of phobias, addictions, and family problems with the help of online discussion groups? What is this magic? We will put it into words. For sure, it is a true phenomenon that is felt every day.

Much of the information in this book is based on true stories. Our thanks to all of the onliners who shared so openly and enthusiastically. (Delilah always changes the names of her friends to protect the guilty...:) We hope you enjoy this little trip.

::::::::::*reaching for your hand*::::::::::
Delilah

1

What and Where on Earth Is Cyberspace?

:::holding your hand:::

Q. Dear Delilah,
How do I get there, and do I really want to go?
TanTom in San Antonio

A. Dear Tom,
If you have a computer with a modem you are only a phone call
away from the many wonders of cyberspace. Why not check it out?

Cyberspace is a place where you can get your stock quotes anytime you wish or send an instant letter to your daughter in Costa Rica for the price of a local phone call. It's a place where you can link up to a global network of large computers (called the Internet) and browse through files that range in size and power from a recipe for Texas chili (and call your fire department to stand by while you sample this one!) to an entire movie. You can read the online issue of *Playboy* magazine, complete with

1

photos, or discuss politics with someone 2,000 miles away. It's where you can meet Sweet Sue on Monday and take her on a trip to the moon on Friday. It is inside your computer and inside your mind. And there is a seat on the next rocket ship reserved for you!

How do I get on this rocket ship?

To get to cyberspace, you need to connect your computer to another computer or a network of computers that provides access to information, services, or activities. Some of these networks are huge, while others are tiny. They are organized as:

1. Major online services (America Online or AOL, Compu-Serve, Prodigy, Microsoft Network or MSN, etc.)

2. Bulletin board services (BBSs)

3. Internet and the World Wide Web (WWW)

These range in scope from local or regional BBSs linking thousands of people together to vast, global networks linking millions of people together worldwide. Think of that familiar cork board in your office. People can gather there to share information and post notices. And, as anyone who has ever worked in an office knows, one of the most popular hang-outs is the company bulletin board. Online networks are similar. Today there are over 60,000 electronic systems nationwide operated by individuals, businesses, nonprofit organizations, and government agencies. They are open 24 hours a day, seven days a week, and are often free except for the cost of your phone call, though some BBS owners, called *sysops* (short for system operators), may charge a membership fee for more extensive services.

There are several ways to get "connected." You can join a large commercial service, which will give you lots of opportunities to meet other people as well as Internet access, or you can choose a smaller, specialized, even local BBS. Or you can purchase special software (*Netscape, Internet Connection, Superhighway Access,* etc.) that will allow you to link your computer directly to the Internet and eliminate an online service middleman. This last method requires a bit more computer savvy but gets easier all the time as new programs hit the marketplace.

The large online services, like CompuServe, AOL, Prodigy, MSN, GEnie, and Delphi, are probably the easiest to access and navigate but might be the most expensive in the long run. They constantly upgrade their capabilities by purchasing smaller companies that have specialized access tools, and they furnish software that gives you the ability to connect to their networks and the

Internet. MSN comes already bundled into your Windows 95 operating system but, at this writing, offers fewer bells and whistles (though costs a bit less!) than its rivals. America Online, Prodigy, and CompuServe also offer special "Internet only" accounts if you don't want to pay for the extras—the special conferences, graphics, etc.

These networks are so complex they rival the passageways formed by telephone companies and post offices. Yep, cyberspace is a big place. If you are new to computer use, you might feel confused already. But even though it sounds complex, it is really pretty easy to get setup. You can even get necessary software for the large online services prepackaged with many computer magazines in your local bookstore. This is a good way to begin, and they thoughtfully give you some free hours to get you started.

Appendix A at the end of this guide will give you "newbies" a simplified overview of the Internet, but the purpose of this little book is to help you "communicate," not to give you hands-on, step-by-step instruction on using your computer or in-depth definitions of technical terms. We assume you know the basics—how to load software, move files, etc. And if you need help in this area, sign up for a basic computer class or take a look at the many howto books and magazines available. Talk to your computer-literate friends and colleagues, even the salesman at your computer store. People love to share their information.

Why are so many taking this trip? Is it for the E-mail, the chat, or the library?

There is something for everyone in cyberspace. Activities on your computer service can involve sending or receiving messages (postings and E-mail), live communication (chat) with other people, and finding material in libraries. If you are hoping to make new friends online, you will need to quickly master this new art of letter writing or "online messaging." If you join a service that provides forums for live chat, you will learn to be witty and quick on your fingers. And if you are interested in online research, you will love exploring files of facts, pictures, sounds, and anything else that can be transformed into the binary code of zeroes and ones that computers understand. When all of this information is reduced to computer code, it can be sent over phone lines using modems and downloaded into your own computer. The speed at which data can move is called *bandwidth*. Fiber-optic cables will soon move this information even faster and allow computer owners to move whole movies into their systems in seconds.

A real value to the online environment is the communities that form around special interests. There are BBSs that offer everything from tips on what to feed your pet boa constrictor to the latest quilting patterns to piles of computer programs. And whatever your interest, you can find your niche. How about joining a BBS called CinemaNet or Smartnet? There are ChuckleNet, Biznet, Friendsnet, and even special "adults only" networks such as After Dark and Throbnet. The Sierra Network offers interactive games, in which you can agree to play checkers with someone 1,000 miles away and chat with him or her at the same time.

This guide is concerned primarily with communication, both interactive (real-time) and asynchronous (a Greek derivation meaning "not at the same time"), where someone can type a message, send it off, and pick up the recipient's response at a later time. Both ways of communicating can be effective in making new friends. A Dallas onliner, known only as TallTexan, insists the best communication mixes "bidness" with pleasure. He owns a travel agency and uses an online service that lets him network for business by posting travel tips as he chats informally with people all over the country.

Now let's take a close look at the art of online messaging.

Messages (postings and E-mail)

A huge attraction to an online service is the ability to exchange mail—called electronic mail, or *E-mail*. Mail can be sent to one specific person or to a whole group. Messages on a specific topic can even be relayed, or "echoed," to all of the BBSs carrying this topic. This is like a worldwide party line. Tracy LaQuey, in her book *The Internet Companion*, tells of a teacher who had her students in the United States communicate with students in the former Soviet Union. "I was deeply moved by a romantic exchange of notes on springtime in our city and springtime in the Ukraine between a young girl with cerebral palsy and a young man whose name was Albert." These two young people remind us that the mind and creative spirit can transcend disabilities and physical limitations. Is it any wonder we are all fascinated with the possibilities? E-mail is a major online activity, so you will want to sharpen your letter-writing skills.

THE GAMEBOX

E-mail Roulette—Send the following E-mail message to five individuals you have spotted on your BBS:

"Hi! I'm new to this crazy online world and hope you can help me answer this question—Does the Information Superhighway have any rest stops? If so, where??"

An ongoing dialogue via E-mail as a result of this question will net you 10 points!

Another quick way to get an online conversation going is to tack up, or "post," your own message on the electronic service of your choice. Or you can decide to reply to a message left by someone else. It doesn't even have to be addressed to you. If there are several postings all about a specific topic, or *thread*, you should read enough to make your response interesting and pertinent. Some Internet newsgroups may contain hundreds of messages, so be sure your posting is relevant. Never send an unrelated posting to many different newsgroups. This posting is called *spam* and can make experienced "netters" livid, especially if it's an advertisement for something you're selling. Plan your message carefully and always be polite, even if you are disagreeing. The following messages are samples from a BBS that Delilah uses. They will give you a feeling for the way a conversation online might begin. The first is from Miker, who wants to meet other people interested in biking. Sugarplum and JoJo respond.

> **Subj**: Any Biker Chicks Online?
> **From**: Miker
>
> Would love to talk biker talk to women with same interest. Post your specs, bike meets, scooter type, etc., especially if you go beyond "family style." Will talk about anything pertaining to scooters.
>
> **Subj**: Biker Chick Here
> **From**: Sugarplum
>
> What kind of bike do you ride??
>
> **Subj**: To Sugarplum
> **From**: Miker
>
> I have several. My favorite is my Harley—a candy-red, full-fendered Softail—very "swoopy!"
>
> **Subj**: Vintage Biker Chick
> **From**: JoJo
>
> Marlon Brando started my interest in biking. I loved *On the Waterfront*. Everyone was a biker then. I don't ride, but I was

always a biker's chick. My dream was to learn. I even married and divorced a biker. But I never learned to ride. Do you think it's too late now?

Subj: JoJo—My Kinda Girl!
From: Miker

Believe me, it's NEVER too late.

As you can see, many online services allow their members to make up their own names. Miker's real name might well be Herbert, but a biker will get more interest from the ladies with "Miker." These made-up monikers define what you want your online persona to be and should be carefully thought out. Screen names can make a difference in the kind of people you meet online, so we will consider them in more detail in later chapters.

Being anonymous allows people to post whatever they wish, and messages can sometimes be very specific. In fact, online message posting is quickly becoming the new personals column of the phone lines. If you're looking for a particular type of man or woman with whom to establish a relationship, you can define your "dreamdate" very carefully. A clever posting may generate a large and immediate response as it flies over the phone lines to thousands of potential friends. Then you can exchange E-mail with one person or several people and get to know a lot about them without giving away any information about yourself until you are sure you want to. Your online posting travels farther and faster and is read by many more people than any other form of communication. In the following message we can see that HobNail knows what she wants:

Subj: Looking for an on/offline friend
From: HobNail

DWF, age 45, lives in the foothill area—Stockton, CA. I'm new to online service and find it quite interesting. I enjoy outdoor activities. If you are a drug-free, nonsmoker, SWM, 35 or older, give me a holler. I'm available for some nonkinky fun.

And she gets a quick response from Blueskye:

Subj: *Response to New Girl—Hobnail*
From: *Blueskye*

Straight male, 51, looking for friendship with compassionate, passionate woman. I'm a responsive, fun, nongeek and feel that cyber-relationships open new worlds without social barriers. I believe we'll be better for it. Interested? E-mail. Let's get to know each other. Washington D.C. area.

Who knows? Perhaps HobNail and Blueskye will get together and find true happiness. At least they have found a meeting place and an outlet for self-expression that they would not have found a few years ago. In our chapter "Looking for Love?" we take a closer look at love on line. Can one find real-life romance, even marriage, beginning with an online relationship? Awwwww go on. Skip ahead.

You can master online communication in a short time and use it for the fun of meeting new people, to further your business interests, or to join in a serious discussion. And if you wish to reach a specific group of onliners, it can be helpful to single them out. Many online services allow you to search for members by name or interests, and America Online also lets you search by age. Prodigy allows you to search the membership data base by name and location. A well-known writer searched out all the writers on several BBSs and sent them reviews for his new book. Then he was able to establish new contacts in the writing world and publicize his new book at the same time.

Much is made in the media of sexually explicit messages and newsgroup postings in cyberspace. There is plenty of this, and the large commercial services have rules to dissuade users from abusive, profane, or sexually offensive postings. However, this is hard, sometimes impossible, to police. And on the Internet, language flows without censorship. We will consider this problem later, but the following posting should make most onliners smile:

Subj: Submissive male, 36, needs lesson
From: Rudy

I am ready to serve. If you need a nude houseboy to do your floors or if you want a boy toy to show off at your next party, I am the one! Perhaps you would like a candlelit dinner and endless body kisses. You would be my only worry. And if I could please you, perhaps I could also have a small degree of pleasure. But that would be for you to say...

Live communication (chat)

The dictionary defines chat as "light, familiar, informal talk." But in cyberspace, chat is lively dialogue typed on one computer and read and responded to almost instantly on another computer. And these computers may be thousands of miles apart, even halfway around the world. You can talk privately to one other person or publicly to many. You can even be invited into a private room where you need a password. There are hundreds of BBSs that provide chat havens, and chatting live online is one of the most popular online activities.

ProStar Plus, in Seattle, Washington, is a 15,000 member BBS that offers international chat links and 400 canned chat actions. You can add sounds and actions to your online words: "sneeze" and "nuke" get used a lot. eWorld is a chat BBS for Macintosh users that includes members from Australia, Canada, New Zealand, and the United Kingdom. It also furnishes sounds that you can insert into your chat, like cheering, booing, laughing, and even quacking. All of the large commercial services,

Delphi, Prodigy, America Online, and Microsoft Network, offer chat forums. CompuServe's answer to the chat board is the CB Simulator. It offers two "bands," the CB General Band and the CB Adult Band. You can click into the Breakfast Club or Lesbian Lifestyles. The Adult Band is closed to those members under 18 years of age. The Computron BBS in Birmingham, Alabama, offers games along with the chat and features Internet E-mail and newsgroups.

It is a fact that these chat boards can occasionally lead to offline business and pleasure contacts. And all commercial services have a set of rules to dissuade users from abusive, profane, or sexually offensive chat, just as they do for message postings. Once more, it is hard to police.

It is true that many chat boards are filled with the frivolous or sexual innuendo. This can be entertaining, and we will cover this type of chat in some detail in upcoming chapters. But some BBSs are very serious. Environet, a chat BBS based in San Francisco, is the official BBS of Greenpeace. Here, you can participate in conferences about animal rights and alternative energy. You can download files of current newsletters and research important environmental issues. In fact, there are probably more serious discussions in the BBSs that offer chat rooms than most people realize.

After the tragic bombing of the Alfred P. Murrah Federal Building in Oklahoma City, there were many online conference rooms filled with people chatting live. Delilah's friend Jim was able to share his personal experience of being only blocks away from the explosion and on his way to that building when it happened. He recounted the feeling of his pickup truck being suddenly halted by the shock wave of the blast and his horror as he realized what he had narrowly escaped. During the weeks and months following, he found his online friends to be supportive and sympathetic as he worked through his feelings of despair and rage at the loss of many friends and acquaintances. "It was very beneficial to have people outside my family and community willing to talk to me about all this," he told Delilah. "We here in Oklahoma needed to know that the world cared about what we were going through."

The following live conversation about the tragedy took place in a chat room and helps us to understand how important online communication can be in sharing news about things that affect us deeply:

BEARCUB:	You know, there were hundreds and hundreds of volunteer fire fighters who went to OKC to help in any way they could...
TXJack:	There was a group from TX who took their vacation time to go.
OKJIM:	They worked round the clock, and everyone got a rose on his bed when he went to bed...
BEARCUB:	Men and women—everyone pitched in, very moving...
OKJIM:	And crime was down in OKC—not one case of looting or vandalism. This tragedy touched EVERYONE!
JudyinFLA:	Jim, how did they feed all these extra people?
OKJIM:	Again, volunteers pitched in with food, and they set up a big dining hall in the convention center...caterers set up trucks all over too...
TXJack:	Long after the rest of the country has moved on, you people in OK will still be dealing with this...
JudyinFLA:	BUT none of us will ever forget...

Now let's consider our last reason to go online—the libraries.

Libraries

Cyberspace is even more than people messaging and chatting. It is more than fun and games. It is information, about anything and everything. Check out the libraries. CharlieB, an avid onliner, says, "Never ask questions if you don't want to know the answers." But if you do want to know the answers, these libraries are for you.

The libraries on electronic bulletin boards contain files of articles, reports, photography, movies, and even books. Steve Cavrak, from the University of Vermont, says, "This resource is gigantic and is growing larger. If it were an eggplant, we'd be in real danger." All kinds of software and transcripts of online conferences are available. And these libraries may be easiest for you to access from the large online services.

Libraries are organized into sections allowing you to browse, just like walking down the aisle of your city library. You can look for a specific file using a file name, message number, or keyword. For example, if you need a special poem for your online sweetheart, you might find it under "English Poets of the 1800s." And when you find what you want, you can copy it, download it into your own personal system, then send it in an E-mail file to the delight of that special someone. How can she resist you when she reads:

> The sunlight clasps the earth
> And the moonbeams kiss the sea:
> What are all these kissings worth
> If thou kiss not me?
>
> Percy Bysshe Shelley

A word about copyright. Many people mistakenly think that everything is free if they find it on the Internet. This isn't so. Copyright laws have evolved over several centuries and are now being hotly discussed as original works can be copied and sent to thousands of onliners with a computer keystroke. There will no doubt be changes in copyright law as we move into this digital revolution. The *Wall Street Journal* commented that "copyright is easy to break on the Internet and hard to enforce." Much information is indeed in the public domain, but you should be careful about what you use and get the author's permission when possible.

Thousands of libraries publish their indexes on the Internet. This information from universities and county libraries is free. To access these files you need their phone number and telecommunications software (usually included in your modem package). Check the Internet newsgroup COMP.INTERNET.LIBRARY for leads to the best libraries.

The Library of Congress may have the most extensive collection of resource materials available. The Colorado Alliance of Research Libraries offers access to academic and public library online catalogs, current articles, as well as the *Internet Resource Guide*. To get help in finding information you can send E-mail to HELP@CARL.ORG., including the word "help" in your message.

Real-life, or offline, libraries just lend you materials. But online libraries encourage you to interact and donate a file or software package to the system. Sometimes you will be rewarded with free connection time for your contribution.

Are the natives friendly?

You will usually find people online to be very helpful and friendly. If you are like most of us, you will find yourself swept up with the many wonders of online possibilities. You will want to spend hours exploring and talking to your new friends. With so many services and BBSs to choose from, it may even be difficult to decide which to join. You won't be able to sample every one, so to find out what is available, pop into your local bookstore and pick up a magazine or newspaper listing the BBSs, or ask your local computer dealer for help. Commercial online services such as CompuServe, America Online, and Prodigy may even provide lists of the smaller BBSs. The online community can be wonderful, with genuine sharing and caring. Let's look at some examples of this.

Is it true what I've heard?

Martha: Can my online friends become as important as my
          real-life friends? I can't wait to talk to them every
          day. Does anyone else feel this way?

Sara: I know what you mean. I feel the same way. In fact,
          sometimes I like my online friends better. They listen
          when I have something important to say.

Martha: And they accept us as we are.

Are genuine friendships formed online? They are! Cyberspace may be a crowded place, but people can feel a real sense of community. Communication in the form of E-mail or conferences or even live chat reinforces this. And more often than you might think, online messages take a serious tone. During the January 1994 earthquake in California many people used their computers to locate each other and send messages of encouragement. Nathan Cobb of the *Boston Globe* reported that "thousands of Californians and non-Californians helped to relay messages to friends and relatives who were unreachable when long-distance phone service was curtailed...Computers were able to go this week where voice telephones temporarily couldn't."

"This is the first time I've really felt that people were linking up—in the truest sense—by computer," said a schoolteacher in St. Louis who had spent hours on his computer talking to people in California. "I hate to sound ridiculously corny, but it was really people helping people."

> **Subj:** Still shaking!
> **From:** All Shook Up
>
> Hi. Mari here. I live in the San Fernando Valley and am still with-
> out utilities except occasional phone service. I am on the last fif-
> teen minutes of laptop battery now, so can't post more for awhile.
> Lots of damage here; some neighbors lost walls and other struc-
> tures. Fortunately, my home is fairly sound on the outside—just all
> the stuff on the inside is broken! But we are doing fine, getting by
> on cold pork and beans and warm sodas—happy to be alive and
> well and riding out the aftershocks as much as possible. How is
> everyone else? Please check in and let us know!!!

Sometimes a posting can even mean life or death. This touching message was circulated through America Online:

> **Subj:** Bone Marrow Transplant
> **From:** Concerned
>
> Alexandra is a 3 1/2-year-old girl of Philippine/Caucasian descent
> who has leukemia. She is in desperate need of a bone marrow
> transplant, which can give her a second chance for life. If you are,
> or someone you know is, of Asian/Caucasian (preferably
> Philippine/Caucasian) descent and want to give her that chance,
> please contact the National Bone Marrow Program at
> (800)Marrow-2. Donors must be between 18 and 55 years of age
> (male or female). Due to Alexandra's racial mix, the donor pool of
> potential matches is extremely small. Many people are needed to
> be type-matched in order to find a suitable donor.

We hope that Alexandra was able to find the help she needed. Her message touched thousands of hearts. As you can see, people have discovered in this new medium a way of expressing their deepest feelings and concerns. Let's consider once more the bombing in Oklahoma that shocked our nation. The following poignant E-mail came from the Wade twins in Oklahoma City on the 26th of April, 1995:

> Dear Delilah,
> I'm writing to you because my brother and I wanted you to

know what it was like as we stood quietly, looking at a scene right out of Dante's "Inferno." We had just delivered 10 cases of eggs, 10 gallons of orange juice, and 12 tubes of sausage to City Church, who'd put out a call for food to feed the many volunteers. And as we stood in silence about a half-block away, at the corner of 5th Street, others joined us, watching the heavy cranes lift huge pieces of concrete and steel that must have weighed several tons. Brave men and women worked desperately trying to find survivors. As we observed the sad work going on, my brother said, "Look at that piece of paper floating out of the building." The wind was gusting out of the south, and as I watched, a piece of paper slowly rode the breeze right toward us. It rose, then dipped, finally landing a few feet from us. I reached down and picked it up, wanting so much for it to be a message from one of my friends still inside the torn and broken ruin. But there was nothing on the paper, just a blank page.

"You going to keep that?" my brother asked.

"Yes, I am," I said as I folded it and put it into my pocket.

That paper symbolized for me the empty and helpless feeling many were sharing as they tallied the loss of so many people, people like you and me. People who lived ordinary lives, who worked hard to provide food and clothing and make a living. These were people who laughed and cried and had the same problems the rest of us have. They were husbands and wives, parents and grandparents. Some were old and some were young and some were very young. And now, they were all gone.

We drove home in silence, and when I went back to my office, I put that piece of paper in my desk drawer. You see, for me it isn't blank at all. It says everything.

Thanks for listening,

J. Wade

Is it more than fantasyland?

Whewwwww! We have begun a whirlwind ride through cyberspace. And by now you know that there is much more than fantasy online. There is indeed something for everyone. And there is always someone anxious to help.

Don't be afraid to explore.

Now call the fire department. It's time for that chili recipe. Didja think we forgot?

Jack Martin's Award Winning Texas Chili

5 lb chili meat—run through course grinder only once. Use either cap meat (top of rib), chuck, or sirloin, and tell your butcher to take out most of the fat and gristle.

Dry Ingredients:
11 Tbsps Adams Chili Powder

1 Tbsp Mexene Chili Blend

2 Tspns Garlic Powder (If using minced garlic, put it into meat while browning.)

2 Tspns Cayenne Pepper

1 Tspn Paprika (Use Mexican style, not Hungarian.)

1 Tbsp Cumin (Ground type)

1/8 Tspn White Pepper

1/4 Tspn Allspice

2 Tspns Salt

1 Tspns MSG (or Accent)

Blend the following until liquefied:
1 8 oz can tomato sauce

1 10 oz can Rotel tomatoes with green chilies

3 medium onions

Also:
1 can heavy beer—not light type

3 jalapeño peppers (slit along sides to let juice escape into meat)

Directions:
Brown chili meat until gray, about 30 minutes. Add blended onions and cook 30 minutes. Add tomato sauce and blended Rotels. Add heavy beer. Cook for 45 minutes more. Then add dry ingredients, stirring slowly. Cook 1 more hour, then squeeze the juice from the jalapeños and throw the peppers away. This is done

using a spatula to squeeze them against the side of the pan so as not to get seeds in chili. Bring up to high heat, and strain grease off top of chili. Eat and enjoy!

Thanks, Jack!

2

Where Do I Fit In?

:::counseling patience:::

Q. Dear Delilah,
What kind of an online name gets the most attention?

Johnny R. in CA

A. Dear Johnny,
Depends on WHAT kind of attention you want. A name to help you find an online friend should tell something about your interests. If you're the out-of-doors type, you could choose "JeeperJohn." If you're looking for cybersex and are outrageous, you might enjoy "9injohnny."

What should I call myself?

Many online services or BBSs allow subscribers to choose screen names that are different from their own. And some allow more than one screen name at a time. If a subscriber wishes to open several accounts, he can have a dozen screen names. If several people in a family are using the service, each can dream up an individual "handle" and secret password.

There can be many reasons for the names people choose. Are you looking for an amorous adventure? You can create a name that will attract people to your good looks or endowments (real or imagined!). TALLNHNDSM would get the attention of the ladies in a room, and BUSTY would have the men smiling. Perhaps you want to use your own initials or first name. Or you might choose a name with historical or celebrity relevance. DELILAH has given a hundred haircuts! And FANCPANTS gets smiles from everyone she meets. GEMINI is a twin, and FIGURE8 ice skates her way all over cyberspace, describing her little spins and twirls.

But whatever you call yourself, it is the first impression people have of you, so make it count. If it is too numeric or too long, it won't be remembered. And our names often open up an online dialogue, so be real sure you want to talk about "bobitizing"—a lot—if you call yourself OL'Bobbit. One online friend even insisted that he would have his handle registered as his very own trademark. "It works like magic with the ladies!" Now we can't use it in this book…:)

THE GAMEBOX

Namegame—Dream up seven wild names to use online and try one a day. When you find the ONE that works, gets attention, and feels right, adopt it and don't look back…:)

If you use your online service for business—and there is a rapidly expanding marketplace online—your descriptive name can act as an advertisement. It can help people remember you when they need your services and enable you to network easily. Consider the screen name TAXES4U. Would you notice this accountant? We bet you wouldn't be surprised to learn that SNAPS is a photographer. An attorney, CHEEPLAW, tells us that he has gotten business just through his descriptive and humorous name posted in the directory of his online service. Everyone notices an attorney with an obvious sense of humor...:)

Your screen name can also reflect your more serious side. If you want to visit a newsroom forum to discuss current events, a name that reflects your expertise could give weight to your comments. What do you think about a person with the name BABYDR? If a physician with DR in his name makes a comment about health care, he will get more attention.

Do I have to tell the truth?

No, you don't have to tell the truth, but there is a distinction between exaggerating, or telling a half-truth, and telling an out-and-out lie that can hurt or deceive your new friends. Delilah believes that the majority of people are honest online, most of the time. "Man is least himself when he talks in his own person. Give him a mask, and he will tell you the truth." This quote from Oscar Wilde seems particularly apt when we think about computer communication. Could this even be the secret to the exploding popularity of computer communication? Under our clever online disguises, we can happily, usually honestly, explore everything and say anything.

Histories or Profiles

Many BBSs and large services allow members to create a profile or thumbnail sketch of background information, and some honesty is needed here. This allows everyone to know something about each other. Some information is private, of course, so you can be billed. And some information is public and can be used by other onliners to search for specific groups or individuals. Truthful profiles make possible a directory search for everyone on your service who enjoys a particular activity—say, running—or is a particular age—say, over 50. If you fit the qualifications, you could be on an energetic onliner's list to receive his newsletter geared to those over 50 who plan on running a 10K race.

Sometimes this background information is so outrageous it is obviously untrue. Does anyone really live in Disneyland? And sometimes information is so brief it is irrelevant. Sometimes facts can be slanted to give a certain impression. Watch out for the married man who tells the ladies he is "separated" from his wife. He probably means since breakfast. Hmmmmmm...what do you suppose he's looking for? More about these sneaky, married scoundrels later...:)

The fantasy world online is very appealing. Everyone likes to pretend. And if your online service gives you the opportunity to create a history or profile, you can even give yourself a different personality from the one you have in the real world. Take time to provide some information about yourself. There are those online who say they won't waste time chatting with someone who has provided no profile at all, and this bit of information saves time with introductions. Of course, if you are using several names, you can make several different profiles. WILD-HORSES likes to have one profile that is purely fictional and humorous and one that advertises his bicycle shop.

On some services you may list your hobbies. These hobbies or interests are a good way to begin a friendship. If someone has listed "hunting" as a hobby and you have a genuine aversion to hunting, this might not be someone with whom you wish to spend your online time.

However, if Thai cooking is a passion with you and you find a person with some expertise in this area, a real bond can form. Perhaps hobbies are your interest, as they are for Modler, who owns a hobby shop in Wisconsin. She met TRAINer online, a model train buff, and they formed a loving relationship. They met in real life at the Hobby Show in Chicago and hope to marry in the near future!

Some of the most entertaining profiles to read are those that have been dreamed up to go with a screen name and are pure fantasy. If you are clever—and our tips should help—you can have lots of fun online. Alice is a good example:

Screen name:	SPEEDRACR
Profile:	
name	Alice
sex	female
state	Texas
birthday	my bidness
computer	nope
occupation	mechanic
hobbies	working on my 1965 Corvette; driving faaast
quote	"Real women prefer a stick shift!"

Don't you think it would be fun to get to know this woman? In reality, she is a quiet and rather shy English teacher and mother of four young children. But when she sits down to chat online, she can be anything she wants. It is a wonderful diversion from our everyday world.

This is an accurate picture of one of Delilah's friends:

Screen name:	CowboyHart
Profile:	
name	Mike
sex	male
state	Montana

birthday	5/25/42
computer	IBM
occupation	software stuff
hobbies	horses, fishing, hunting
quote	not interested unless you can do it from a horse

And this New York policeman is well-known online:

Screen name:	TOP DRAWER
Profile:	
name	Ted
sex	male
state	New York
birthday	Gemini
computer	Pentium
occupation	police officer
hobbies	photography, computers, reading, motorcycles
quote	"Survival is the key."

Quotations

Clever, even wild, quotations from others can add a lively aspect to an online personality. A quotation can be a tool to open both minds and hearts when you are typing to your cyberfriends, and they are used often. Sometimes they are from famous people, and sometimes they are all ours, a window to our own honesty and humor. What would you think an individual was saying with the quotation, "Wrap your thighs around my eyes." Or how about, "If it is to be, it is up to me." Here are some favorite quotations from online friends:

"Romantic at heart. I can't help it. I believe in knights in armor and princes, but lately all the princes have been toads."

"Enjoy life. This is not a rehearsal."

"The love doctor is always in—in trouble most of the time."

"Life is short, and life is long."

"You need it and I have it."

"When I'm good, I'm very good. But when I'm bad, I'm even better!"

"Try me...no tellin' who I am today."

"It's not conflict that causes war, but the insistence that conflict be resolved."

"Good judgment comes from experience, and experience comes from bad judgment."

"The higher up you climb on the ladder of success, the more people there are that see your underwear."

"Choose your friends by observing how they treat others who can do them no good."

"The smallest good deed is better than the grandest intention."

"You always miss the shots you do not take."

"Aging is mandatory but maturity is optional."

Suppose you have met a group of friends online you enjoy chatting with. You enjoy their funny screen names (or "scream" names as one onliner calls 'em) and you know something about them—where they really live and perhaps what their occupations are. How much actual information can you comfortably divulge about yourself?

Who can I trust?

This is not usually a real problem, but there are some basic guidelines for these beginning stages of online sharing. Delilah would advise you to NEVER make your full name and city available to everyone who looks at your profile. And give out your phone number with great care. (Unless, of course, you are DUSTY in Las Vegas and have a 900 number for "business.") Always be careful about giving out any personal information online until you really know your new friends. We will talk a bit more about online dangers later.

Watch out for gender benders. These are people who enjoy pretending to be men when they are women or vice versa. Changing hats can give you a whole new perspective on communication between men and women, but it is a bit dishonest if you engage in a serious conversation with someone.

You should also be prepared for a group online that enjoys sending shocking, sexually explicit messages or material to the unsuspecting. Some recipients find these notes amusing, but others don't. The senders are usually in their teen years and are easily deterred with a snappy reply like, "I'm gonna tell your Momma!" On America Online, these writers are called "snerts." The cry "SNERT ALERRRRT" is heard at all times of the day and night, in both public and member rooms.

"I signed on once using my daughter's name, just to see what kind of messages women get online," said Ed A., "and was I ever shocked."

Nikki quickly added, "I used to fire a message right back to a joker like that telling him where I thought he should go. But now I just ignore the oniners I don't care for. And they stop sending those crazy messages if you don't reply."

"Oh come on, guys. That's part of the online fun! I like to see how wild some people can be," said Joan from New Jersey. "There is room for everyone in cyberspace!"

Delilah believes that a person's true nature is magnified online. If he is a caring individual in real life, he will be very caring online and happy to spend time discussing a problem, or policing and protecting the online community from ne'er-do-wells. And the shady real-life character is the oniner who is secretly married or the one stealing passwords or sending lewd and offensive messages to the newbies who haven't yet learned to shut him off. All in all, the online community is just a digitized expression of the real world.

Does anyone care?

Don't be fooled by the fluff and silly stuff. There is real caring, friendship, even love online. Hiding behind an anonymous persona and a fictional name can do amazing things to people as they learn to communicate over the wires. It can bring out our caring natures in a way telephone conversations can't. Voices online seem to whisper. There is no accent, no inflection, no pitch to feed your built-in prejudices. There are only written words, quickly composed and hastily typed. There are mistakes and misspellings. And there is also TRUTH. Most people find it easy to explore their deeper thoughts, dreams, hopes, even fantasies in this new and unusual interactive cyber-pub. Online, there is always a "bartender" eager to listen.

Experienced online chatters insist they can read between the lines. It takes a lot of hours of online chatting to understand this, to read the clues in online play and learn how to communicate in a deeply mental way. It's an almost physical phenomenon. This guidebook should help you understand what your new friends are really saying. Consider their speed of typing, spelling, words chosen, symbols, or emoticons (check our list in the next chapter) and use your own intuition. You may feel yourself make an actual mental connection. No, your keyboard won't get hot and your monitor won't cast an eerie glow. But something will happen. And if you suddenly find a relationship blossoming with a particular friend, give it lots of typetime. Ask many questions, like what your friend is wearing or for a description of the room where he or she is sitting. Even ask what your pal had for lunch. Get as complete a mental picture as you can, and, over a period of time, you will find that you are beginning to understand this person's intellect. You will be able to anticipate your mindmate's words and sense a mood or state of mind. If you continue and become closer and closer, there will be genuine caring that just might develop into a new kind of love—cyberlove. Relax, let it happen, and enjoy this remarkable experience. "Cyberlove with a special someone is what everyone chatting online is looking for," says Hugh in Indiana. We will take a closer look at love online later.

Support groups

Online support groups are flourishing. Psychiatrists and psychologists are exploring this new medium and even holding group discussions online. All the major online commercial services provide forums to discuss everything from sexuality and relationships to addiction and obsession. There are groups for the parents of terminally ill children and sites for gay and lesbian youth. Reid Fishler, founder of the Youth Assistance Organization on the Internet, started a site for young people to openly discuss their sexuality. There are many such forums. And sometimes a computer screen may be the only thing a person has to turn to in a time of desperation. Social workers praise the existence of Internet bulletin boards that provide help for so many.

One very popular room on America Online is called "The Friends of Bill W." All those familiar with Alcoholics Anonymous will recognize this as a safe room, where one may talk about the problems of alcohol abuse. Questions are carefully answered and support is freely given. Often phone numbers are exchanged and real-life friendships form. Make no mistake, this is genuine caring.

How does a relationship begin?

Patti and Lucky7's story follows. It should help you understand how an online relationship can develop. Relationships can grow over a period of days, weeks, even years. But Patti and Lucky may be on the fast track. In this story you will see that several conversations can go on at once, and as you follow the dialogue, remember that spelling doesn't count when you are involved in an interesting exchange...:)

CHAT LIVE—A Story

The muscles across her shoulders relaxed as she pushed her chair away from the computer. Pat had been tapping on the keys for hours, doing "mega" spreadsheets for her company. Stretching her arms, she wondered if HE was online yet. Time-outs to chat with others on the computer were becoming the best part of her days. And anonymous "adult chat" forums on the telecom service attracted many participants. A number of these people were interested primarily in talking about sex, but sometimes it was fun to get into a light conversation. After a stressful day, they seemed like her friends.

Everyone in the system had a code name. She was "Patti." She had met an interesting man a week ago who was called "Lucky7," and she felt she was getting to know lots about him. They had chatted every afternoon at 4:30 and she was looking forward to another conversation.

Quickly logging onto ChatLine, she kicked her pumps off and settled back to relax.

OnlineGuide: ***You are in "Hall B"***
Christa800: Yeah, I took the tram up and walked down...
WayneR234: Was it lovely?
Lucky7: **Hi there...**
Patti: **Hi...**
Fireman: Do any girls here wanna have fun?
Lucky7: **You're lookin good tonite, Patti.**

AUTOMAN:	Hi, candy.
Patti:	**So are you, you LUCKY guy.**
WayneR234:	How old are you, Christa?
Lucky7:	**How were things in the office today?**
Patti:	**About as usual. Is it HOT in your office?**
Christa800:	<————over 21
Lucky7:	**Always…**
Patti:	**It was hot here today…**
Lucky7:	**Wanna get a beer and cool off [_]?**
Patti:	**(((((Lucky7)))))—hugs to you!**
CandyB:	Have we met, AUTOMAN?
Patti:	**What did you do today?**
Lucky7:	**The day's not over…**
Patti:	**I mean for work?**
Lucky7:	**Oh! I pounded these computer keys as usual. U?**
AUTOMAN:	Ha! Since when did that matter?
Patti:	**Same ol, same ol…just killing time until I can leave…**
Lucky7:	**How long on chat live?**
Patti:	**About 6 mo.**
Lucky7:	**People are interesting…**
Patti:	**Some are…**
Lucky7:	**LOL (Laughing Out Loud)**
Patti:	**How old are you?**
Lucky7:	**37. U?**
Patti:	**28**
CandyB:	Let's play truth or dare
Lucky7:	**Wanna go into a private room?**
Patti:	**OK**
Lucky7:	**Meet me in the "Casino"**

With a few quick keystrokes, Pat scrolled through the rooms listed and tapped into the private room "Casino." Her terminal was quietly whirring and she glanced up to see the late afternoon sunrays slant through her window. Now they could talk without interference from the other chatters, but it was almost time to leave the office.

OnlineGuide:***You are in "Casino"***
| **Lucky7:** | **Took you awhile** |

Patti:	I had to go through several rooms. You like to gamble?
Lucky7:	Sometimes. Where were we? Oh yeah. Tell me about yourself. What do you look like?
Patti:	You first…
Lucky7:	I'm 6'2", 200#, brown hair and eyes. U?
Patti:	I'm 5'6", blonde hair, blue eyes, slim
Lucky7:	Married?
Patti:	Are you?
Lucky7:	No
Patti:	Me neither
Lucky7:	Ever fool around? Just kidding…
Patti:	Ohhhh, look at the clock! Sorry gotta go. Time to go home…
Lucky7:	Running away? See you tomorrow?
Patti:	Sure, why not…

Smiling to herself, she began to gather her things. These guys were so predictable. One could always just log off. No real identities needed to be exchanged, no relationships formed, unless the participants wished to pursue the matter. Pat knew that sometimes people did exchange phone numbers and even meet each other. But that was one trip she didn't intend to take. How could you ever be sure that someone was telling the truth. This guy could be a mass murderer. She smiled again. Somehow that didn't seem to fit. Snapping off her desk lamp, she hurried toward the door. She would just make the 5:22 train.

THE NEXT DAY

OnlineGuide:	***You are in "ThirtyPlus"***
Lucky7:	Hello, again
Patti:	Hi
DaisyDuke3:	Hi, everyone!
Lucky7:	BRB—don't leave! (BRB=be right back)
Patti:	What are you doing?
DANNO33:	Is anyone in this room over 25? Really?
Lucky7:	Finishing some work. Whatcha wanna do tonight?
Patti:	Whatever you want…
Lucky7:	REALLY?

DaisyDuke3:	*I definitely am over 30…:)*
Patti:	**What do you have in mind?**
Lucky7:	**Meet me in private room—FEVER**
OnlineGuide:	***You are in "FEVER"***
Lucky7:	**Are you alone?**
Patti:	**Yes. What's your real name?**
Lucky7:	**Ted. Come sit next to me. What's your real name?**
Patti:	**My name is Pat—truth**
Lucky7:	**:::: holding your hand:::: soft hands**
Patti:	**Do you think people ever really get together after meeting online?**
Lucky7:	**Some do!**
Patti:	**Are people honest?**
Lucky7:	**Why not? Most people are looking for some-one.**
Patti:	**Are you lonely?**
Lucky7:	**Not now ::::::kissing you gently:::::**
Patti:	**Time to leave—sorry. Tomorrow?**
Lucky7:	**I'm not very lucky in my timing…LOL (laugh-ing out loud) I'll be here at 4:30, and I'll describe a kiss from me to you…**

Pat sat for a few minutes in front of her darkened screen. If only life could be that simple. If only she really did have a Ted in her life.

As she hurried toward the elevator, she noticed the tall man who had just transferred to her floor. She had heard he was some sort of computer whiz. He would probably try to change their proce-dures. Well, he would soon find out how stuck in the routines most of the programmers were. Maybe she should introduce herself. Everyone called him Theodore, Ted for short…

3

What Language Do They Speak in Cyberspace?

:::watching you learn the words::: ô¿ô

Q. Dear Delilah,
I know that LOL means "laughing out loud" in cyberspeak, but
what does IMHO mean?

HollyHart

A. Dear Holly,
There are hundreds of abbreviations, acronyms (words formed
from the initial letters of other words), and emoticons (those little
symbols that indicate emotions) used in chatting online and new
ones are invented every day. But some are more well known than
others. IMHO means "In My Humble Opinion." And IMHO, COITOF!
(Chatting Online is Tons of Fun!)

The language used in communication, often referred to
as "cyberspeak," "netspeak," or "computalk," varies from
group to group. For instance, Prodigy members use <G>
for <grin> more often than America Onliners do, where
the smilie :) is happily in vogue. We will consider a list of
terms used online, but there are some general guidelines

that we should look at as well. These guidelines are followed fairly carefully by onliners, and although an inadvertent mistake won't ruin your online reputation forever, you will want to be comfortable and relaxed as soon as possible so that you won't be an obvious newbie and can concentrate on having fun with your cyber-pals.

Can I send a :) to my boss?

NO. There is a definite difference between communicating online for pleasure and communicating for business. If you are sending an E-mail message to your co-workers, or even, <gasp>, your boss, smilies and abbreviations are usually inappropriate. Many people get hundreds of E-mail messages daily, and they don't have the time or humor to deal with your QPs (cute pictures).

Several very big mistakes to watch out for where E-mail is concerned include sending a private message to

the whole company—<DG> (double gasp)—writing a message so poorly that it is misunderstood, and forwarding your favorite jokes and frivolous newsgroup mailings to work associates who really don't want them.

It is also a universal truth that entire messages should not be typed in capital letters, either for business or for pleasure. If you use CAPS often, you come off as heavy-handed or rude. You are shouting. CAPS also make messages harder and slower to read. Keep your CAPS lock key for emphasis, as the following example will illustrate. Can you tell which message is business and which is pleasure?

To: Ms. Goodbody
From: Mr. Eisner

Please note that the meeting scheduled for 12:30 P.M. TODAY must be changed to 1:30 P.M., due to an unforeseen conflict. Please advise your secretary.

To: My Fav Good Body,
From: @^@

Soooo sorry, but lunch in my private office must be changed to 1:30 today, due to a surprise visit by the MRS!!! Tell your secretary to hold your calls! :))

Is it coool to send a flame?

Some onliners enjoy sending flames (nasty or angry messages) to others; some enjoy getting flamed, and if it is to encourage a lively debate, it can even be acceptable. A heated debate can be a wonderful form of self-expression and should not be discouraged. But a clever, whimsical comment can sometimes look like a rude insult and can quickly escalate into inappropriate and emotional behavior. Adults who would never raise their voices in face-to-face conversation can find themselves participating in verbal tantrums, raging at someone else across the cyber-miles. Spontaneous exchanges were never more powerful.

Why does this happen? Perhaps it is the anonymity of online communication. Sometimes targets don't seem like real people. And remember that in this new world it is easy to misjudge another person. Flamers are often mild-mannered and quiet in real life but enjoy retaliating against those in power when they get to a keyboard. And, interestingly, although flamers are often men, women also feel very empowered online. They feel more open to express themselves politically, personally, AND sexually. They can flame with the best of 'em. Sometimes flame-throwers crave attention and hope for a hot, defensive reply, but don't let the force of the online medium sweep you away. No matter how clever or inventive a mean missive may be, consider your urge to participate very carefully. Once you've reacted, you can't take back what you've said. Don't put in writing what you don't want thrown back at you. The best way to deal with a hurtful flame-thrower is to ignore him. A good rule of thumb is to try to see your messages through your readers eyes.

Conferences usually have moderators who try to keep the discussion on a specific topic and defuse online fights. MerryBell entered a conference on alcoholism late and misunderstood what was being discussed. She felt the comments made were directly about her and was angry at her friends for talking about her behind her back. Luckily, LittleBareOne had been logging, or recording the discussion and was able to upload it to her so that she could see they had not been talking about her specifically.

If you find yourself in a personal conflict online, E-mail may not be the best communication tool to use. You might want to engage on a deeper level where feelings are concerned and pick up the phone. We tend to be more careful and thoughtful when voices are heard. Also, a phone call is more private and secure.

How will your online words tell your friends what you

really mean? Online language—the emoticons and abbreviations—will help. Adding a frown :(or a smilie :) to the end of a sentence will convey what you are feeling. And when you see emoticons on your screen you will be able to tell when someone is trying to amuse you with a wink ;) or hugging you in affection {{{{you}}}}. With a bit of practice, you will be able to tell when someone is really trying to find a friend or just playing for a few minutes. In fact, the more experience you have online, the more fine-tuning you will be able to do. Perhaps you are in the mood to share a good joke or perhaps you are tempted by Apilot, who suggests cybersex in an airplane at 30,000 feet. All of these online games are greatly enhanced with emoticons and abbreviations. They are much more than just cute little "pictures."

As we have said, it is also very helpful to forget about spelling and punctuation when typing madly to your computer partner. Timing is important: if you have to check your dictionary, you will miss the point. Remember, adding extra letters to a word gives it more meaning. "What" can become "Whattt?" And extending the word "very" raises eyebrows considerably. *(Are you verrrry pretty?)*

What are the latest shorthand symbols, abbreviations, and acronyms?

A novice to computer communication should spend time learning the online language as quickly as possible. It's easy and fun. You want to make the best impression. And dropping a few of these into your conversation will tell everyone you are clever, witty, and quick on your fingers.

It is amazing how personalities come through with just words on a screen. You can tell a cynic from an extrovert and a flirt from a sophisticate. Notice how symbols, acronyms, and abbreviations help our understanding in the following examples:

oh yeaahh? YRS (cynic)

OH YEAH! <G> (extrovert)

ohhh yeah? :) (flirt)

Oh yes! (sophisticate)

SittnPretty uses an arrow to emphasize that she is having a special day:

SittnPretty: <——— celebrating her birthday :)

Jake202 is "showing" us what he is doing:

Jake202: ::::::::singing with full voice::::::

and Maria is shouting—maybe to SittnPretty??

Maria: HAPPY B-DAY

Abbreviations and acronyms

The following terms are widely accepted in mainstream conversations online because they have been used for years. And you can make up your own as well. An asterisk indicates the most common:

*AFK:	Away From Keyboard
*BAK:	Back At Keyboard
BBW:	Big Beautiful Women, or Beautiful Black Women
BL:	Belly Laughing!
*BRB:	Be Right Back

*BTW:	By The Way
CUAOP:	Cracking Up All Over the Place
C U l8r:	See You Later
DIKU:	Do I Know You?
DUMKYH:	Does Your Momma Know You're Here? (asked in humor)
FAQ:	Frequently Asked Questions
FOCL:	Falling out of Chair Laughing
FWIW:	For What It's Worth
*f2f:	Face To Face
*GAL:	Get A Life!
G,D&H:	Grinning, Ducking & Hiding!!
G,D&R:	Grinning, Ducking & Running!!
GIGO:	Garbage In, Garbage Out
*GMTA:	Great Minds Think Alike
+:	Great Minds Think Alike (abbreviated)
HNIDWTGP:	Hell, No! I Don't Want To Go Private!
HOUEW:	Hanging On Your Every Word
*IC:	I See!
IKWUM:	I Know What You Mean
*ILY:	I Love You
*IM:	Instant Message (popular on America Online)
*IMHO:	In My Humble Opinion
IOW:	In Other Words
KMYF:	Kiss Me You Fool
KWIM:	Know What I Mean?
KWTII:	Know What Time It Is? (as in, Is it late?)
*LOL:	Laughing Out Loud

NUL:	No! You're Lying
OGKT:	Only God Knows That!
***OIC:**	Oh, I See
OMG:	Oh, My Gosh!
OTOH:	On The Other Hand
PITA:	Pain In The Ass!
PNCAH:	Please, No Cussing Allowed Here!
***:::Poof::::**	Out of Here (signing off now)
POW:	Problem Older Woman
PTMM:	Please Tell Me More!
ReHi!:	Hi Again!
RI:	Romantic Intent
***ROF:**	Rolling On The Floor (often connected with LOL)
***ROFLMAO:**	Rolling On The Floor, Laughing My Ass Off
ROFL&CGBU:	Rolling On The Floor Laughing & Can't Get Back Up
***S/A C:**	Sex, Age Check
SGAL:	Sheesh, Get a Life!
SIBU!HH:	Sure! I Believe You! Ha! Ha! (really nonbelief)
SIWIIMV:	Sorry! I Was In Instant Message-ville!
TNTL:	Trying Not To Laugh!
***TTFN:**	Ta-Ta For Now
TTKSF:	Trying To Keep Straight Face!
UAPITA:	You're A Pain In The Ass!
WDUGU:	Why Don't You Grow Up?
WTGP:	Want To Go Private?
WUF:	Where You From?
YIU:	Yes, I Understand!
YIWGP:	Yes! I Will Go Private!

*YRS:	Yeah! Right! Sure!
YSWUS:	Yeah! Sure! Whatever You Say! (said in disgusted nonbelief)

These are handy if you want to explore the D/s or S/M games online (more about these games later):

SWMBO:	She Who Must Be Obeyed (Domme)
HWMBO:	He Who Must Be Obeyed (Dom)

QPs (cute pictures) and surprises

These are usually used when you are having fun or want to get some attention online.

*^5	high five
@	doughnut
[:]	poptart
^v^	bird or bat
~	tongue
[_]>	beer mug
*(_)o	regular coffee cup
(__)0	large coffee cup
{_} $	fancy coffee cup
\-/	iced tea
Y	wine
^=================^	burning candle at both ends
————{————{——@	long-stemmed rose
12x———{——{——@	dozen roses
{ }	hug

*{{{()}}	lots of hugs
*<G>	Grin
<BG>	Big Grin
<VBG>	Very Big Grin
*<BSEG>	Big S—- Eating Grin
<L>	Laughing
??!!	Guess what?
...—...	S.O.S.
ewwww	That's disgusting
word	emphasizes word, as in *love*
#$@%*	expletive

Smilies

These popular little emoticons are widely used and can really set you apart. They add inflection to your typed words. Tip your head 90 degrees to the left to appreciate them:

:D	big grin
:)	smile
:>)	man smiling
:>(	sad face
:)(:	two-faced
;)	wink
#:-)	bad hair day
: #	censored
:p	sticking out tongue
:*	kiss

:p*	French kiss
:)~	French kiss also
: /)	not funny
:—8	talking out of both sides of mouth
: *)	clowning around
:W	whispering or talking softly
B>)	smiling with sunglasses
:X	oops! (covering mouth!)
:-"	whistling
:-&	tongue-tied
<<<{:>	wearing several hats
:-}	wearing lipstick
:pPpPpPpP	giving someone a raspberry
:-J	tongue-in-cheek comment
:-O	"Oh, nooooo!"

People

These are just for fun but sometimes come in handy! Which one do you think CBASS uses whenever he is online? (If you guessed <:)))><, you win!)

O:)	angel
+<:-I	monk or nun
+-(:-)	the pope
C=:-)	chef
@@@@:)	Marge Simpson
*<(:')	Frosty the Snowman

*<l:)	Santa
/:-)	Gumby
}:>	devil
<:)))><	fish
<+)))><	dead fish
————<;)))><	caught fish
>')))><	happy fish
'@;;;;;;;;;	centipede
8)	frog
3:-o	cow
.V	duck
= = = = :}	snake
8 :]	gorilla

Definitions

The following definitions will help you follow an online conversation. Most onliners know these very well, but new ones are invented every day.

Bash	real-life get-together
f	female
Loft	private room
Lurk	to watch the action but not participate
m	male
Newbie	one new to online communication
Punted	to lose your modem connection and disappear from the screen
Snert	one who enjoys shocking others online with sexually explicit messages

Spam	messages unrelated to the topic and usually sent to numerous newsgroups
Take a Walk	go to a private room
Thread	topic being discussed

When a woman and a man find themselves in an online relationship, they may want to formalize this in a monogamous way, have an online pretend marriage ceremony, and become:

OW	Online Wife
OH	Online Husband

If they are married to others in real life, their spouses become...:)

OH in L	Online Husband-in-Law
OW in L	Online Wife-in-Law

X-Rated

These are very special and not always appropriate...:)

(((_!_)))	mooning or shaking your bootie
\(;)/	very naughty
:-0	orgasmic (related to the WAV or sound file {S orgasm, which is the sound of a woman having an orgasm à la *When Harry Met Sally*)
:>)~	feeling oral
FUBR	F—-ed Up Beyond Repair
SNAFU	Situation Normal—All F—-ed up
DILLIGAF	Does It Look Like I Give a F—-?

NFW	No F—-ing Way!
LAB&TUD	Life's A Bitch & Then You Die

Do I need some style?

Those who insist that online communication is about substance, not style, are missing a wonderful layer to online life. In a real-time chat online, people tend to type words as if they are in a conversation. They type the way they really talk. SarahA says, "When I talk to my daughter online, I can actually *hear* her speaking." And in order to embellish your online personality, attract friends, and be remembered, you need to capitalize on your style. You'll have more fun if you let yourself go.

Are you a spunky person? Do you love to have fun? Or are you the shy and mysterious type? What would you *like* to be? Your style online can even reflect a part of your personality that you keep secret in real life. And it will probably just appear naturally as you begin to feel comfortable. If you are clever and quick, your typing might reflect this in speed and your own trademark smilies. Farmerboy always gives a rose @—}—}— to the ladies he chats with. If you are quiet and thoughtful, you might type more slowly and add the more traditional, quiet smilie :) to show you are amused. DevilDom cracks his whip {S whip and winks lewdly };>. SeeSaw never uses any CAPS. She's easy to spot. And Snapper gives lots of {{{{{{{hugs}}}}}}}.

Delilah has an online friend who prefers to watch what others do online rather than join in. This is called *lurking* and can be especially helpful when you are new to a group and need to understand the thread (or subject) before making a comment. However, on many services and BBSs everyone in a chat group can see your name on the screen, and they may wonder why you are lurking and not playing. It is considered impolite to ALWAYS lurk, though voyeurism can be fun from time to time.

Your E-mail signature also reflects your style. Internet signatures usually consist of your address and contact information, but they can also show some personality. You can add a quote or even a picture. Remember to keep it brief, appropriate, and unique.

A signature for Delilah might look like this:

```
        $$$$$$$$$
      $$$$$$$$$$$$$$
    ($$$$$$$$$$$$$$$$$$)        Delilah
    ($$$            $$$)        AskDelilah@aol.com
    ($      ~   ~     $)        "A hard man is good to
    $      O.   .O    $            find...:)"
    | \       /\     / |
    *  \    ( <> )   /  *
         \ ____ _/
          I   I
          ######
```

How can I stay out of trouble? Or do I really want to?

Netiquette (Chat Etiquette)

Throughout this book are tips for safe play online. Don't let the power of the online medium affect your best judgment. There is always a time and place for everything online, and if you want to stir things up, be sure you are not hurtful to someone. Whatever BBS or online service you join will provide a list of rules of behavior. And if your behavior is a tad out of place, you will quickly hear about it. To be safe, treat others as you would like to be treated and you will have no trouble making friends.

Be genuine in what you say online. Don't pretend to be a celebrity. Don't pretend to have an expertise you don't have. You can easily give the wrong impression. And your reputation can spread more quickly than you might believe. Don't lead your friends on and make promises you don't intend to keep. Hawkeyes had such a way with the ladies online (more dates than he could keep!) that he had to change his screen name to avoid many angry E-mails from his jealous online girlfriends. He even had to move from CompuServe to America Online!

Although it is quite free-wheeling on the Internet, it is not a good idea to use profanity in open forums on the commercial services. You may be *poofed,* or taken off the screen. This is called being *TOSed,* or removed under terms of service, on America Online. Your online fantasies should be intricately created and alluring, not crass or crude. Take your cue from what your cyberpartner is writing to you. RobbyT learned this lesson.

> RobbyT: *You don't understand a G— D—- thing about my problem!*
>
> Katherine: *Well, you don't have to get so rude. I was trying to have an intelligent conversation with you, but I don't appreciate that kind of language.*

Always use the system's Good-bye or Logoff command when you are leaving. If you use WAV (sound) files, type {S bye. Don't just hang up. Be polite. Remember that emotions can get amplified in cyberspace, and the most important ingredient in every bulletin board is the people. Treat 'em nicely. The possibilities and realities of human interaction are endless.

The following passage is from a Harlequin* romance novel copyrighted in 1975 and written by Violet

---

*Harlequin® is a registered trademark of Harlequin Enterprises Limited.

Winspear. It is called *Satan Took a Bride* and was plucked off a dusty shelf at the Journey's End Resort outside San Pedro in Belize, where they aren't online yet. Delilah has taken some liberties to show what this passage might look like if it were written on a computer today and posted in alt.stories on the Internet:

> "She stood there still clad in the silk pajama jacket because her clothes had been taken away and no doubt fed to the fishes. <:)))>< Her heart ♥ beat fast and furiously under the dark silk, and she was shockingly aware of her imposture and had to duck .V back into the bed and hide herself. :(
>
> As the Captain swept his stern look over her (õ¿õ), she cast an imploring look (ô¿ô) at Luque de Mayo, who this morning was clad in black Levis and a black, high-throated sweater that made him look like a panther (^..^). He walked with equal silence and suppleness as he came to her and with a single strong movement lifted her, then tossed her back in bed. TOS
>
> 'A Spaniard is either a priest +-(:-) or a devil } :>, and you know what I am, don't you?'
>
> Impulsively he took her lips :} with a sudden savagery, and somehow, in some mysterious way that she was hardly aware of, he changed their positions so that she lay beneath him, pressed into the cushions, at the mercy of his lean, hard, raking strength. :0
>
> Then he wrenched away from her. HWMBO (If you have forgotten what this means, look back at Abbreviations and Acronyms.) "Don't you ever let any other man behave like that with you! You should be whipped. {S whip You're a flirtatious grape-picker ∞∞ with plenty of experience of men and their ways, so sit up, and pull your dress down over your knees! ÕÕ"

And so on and so on...

THE GAMEBOX

Your Trademark—Dream up your own original picture trademark, and use it every time you are online with your new friends. Make it simple and easy to type. When someone types it back to you as soon as you log on, you WIN.

4

What Is Cybersex?

:::winking at you::: ô¿~

Q. Dear Delilah,
What is it, and how can I get some?

Louis in Kentucky

A. Dear Louis,
The first part of your question is the easiest—ferinstance . . .

Lancelot:	Fantasize that I'm standing behind you at your computer. Don't turn around. My hands lay gently on your shoulders. Can you feel my warm breath on your neck?
PrincessLea:	Ohhhh...I do feel someone behind me.
Lancelot:	Unbutton your shirt...
PrincessLea:	You smell like a hot summer night...like musky roses...
Lancelot:	I am touching your bare shoulders...so smooth and silky...now a soft kiss on your warm neck...
PrincessLea:	I turn my head and give your chin a little lick...ummmmmm

Cybersex is the erotic communication between two people as they describe a delicious sexual fantasy to each other on their computers. It is romantic, a bit kinky, sometimes "veryhot," and if the partners are creative typists and clever with words, it can be intensely stimulating. And it's so much more. It is magic.

Computer communication is uniquely seductive. The exciting technology combined with intimate mind connections to anonymous cyberpals can be incredibly powerful. Danny D., a tall, good-looking man in Ohio, calls this magic "cyberbond"—"deep and mental, addictive, magnetic and unstoppable." It gives the term "computer dating" a new dimension.

The first time you log on and go into a chat area, you will probably be happily delighted. People are very open and friendly. You are immediately welcomed, and if you are obviously "f" (female), you may receive a ——{——{—@ (rose). If you are using a service that allows you to pick a screen name that is different from your real name, you will feel free to express yourself more openly, to join in immediately and type whatever you like. A screen name like "James Baud" will get more interest from the others than "Jim Johnson," as you will soon discover. In chat forums geared for adults, sex plays a major role in conversations and quickly becomes very explicit. Amazingly, computer communication can strip away our inhibitions and shyness. The combination of anonymity and freedom from accepted standards of social behavior provides an open playground for adult activities.

What do I say?

To help you better understand what to expect, let's consider in detail what happens in a typical chat room on America Online. (On some BBSs very explicit hot chat is the norm, but on AOL you can find a more mainstream variety.) Our two participants, HoneyB and HansomJack, first meet in a room called "Romance." Their names appear in the room roster in the corner of the screen, along with 20 or so other names. Rooms have a maximum number allowed so that everyone has a chance to participate in the public banter. Conversations can go in any direction and usually include general information like S/AC (Sex/Age Check) or "Where do you live?" The name of the speaker shows on the left side of the screen as his or her words appear.

HoneyB types her "Hi, everyone" into a box at the bottom of her screen, and a keystroke releases her words into the room. Jack loves her name, notices she is new to the room, and quickly searches the profile directory to see what information she has provided. Further interested in her, he whispers to her with an instant message (IM) and a click of his mouse, which appears on her screen only. "Hello. I love your name."

If HansomJack is good at this, he will approach her carefully. An obvious ploy such as "Wanna fool around?" might turn her off. Good openers are "How was your day?" or "My, you look pretty tonight" or "Come here often?" Bad openers are "Let's have sex" or "What's your bra size?" or even "Wanna f——, honey?" Although some online services attempt to censure what is typed, there are no restrictions in the private instant messages that appear only on HoneyB's screen on AOL.

Remember, onliners are all ages and very literate, with good incomes and adventurous spirits. "Watcha wearing?" is often asked and can elicit a wonderfully comic answer.

| HansomJack: | I'm looking good in my fuchsia silk boxers and Air Jordans tonight! |
| HoneyB: | Jack, you dressed! I'm STILL in my old blue bathrobe and my battery powered bunny slippers...:) |

53

> HansomJack: *But you look so cute in a bathrobe!*

And if half of the people "connected" are just there to have fun, the other half, those trying to meet someone special, are also having a good time as they read this public dialogue between HoneyB and HansomJack.

HoneyB likes Jack's compliment and quickly responds "Why, thank you! And you are verrrrry handsome! LOL" She shows him she is not new to online chat by adding *r*'s to "very" for emphasis, and the LOL (laughing out loud) abbreviation indicates a sense of humor and a playful nature.

If the conversation is moving along and interest is building, Jack may ask her to click her mouse several times to join him in a private room. A sexual fantasy develops best in a secret room, where only the two participants see the words typed onto the screen. These rooms can be created by clicking your mouse on the box "Private Room" and then giving this room a special name that no one else will know. They can decide together to create a name for their room based on some common interest they have discovered, or, as in this case, Jack may take the lead and invite her to join him where he is waiting in the private room he has called "Red Corvette."

> HoneyB: *I like your pretty convertible!!*
> HoneyB: *It has a wonderful new-car smell!*
> HansomJack: *And it likes you!*
> HansomJack: *::::settling you into the front seat::::::*
> HoneyB: *Where shall we go?*
> HansomJack: *Let's take a drive up to the point—look at the stars.*
> HansomJack: *::::::shifting into 1st gear:::::: VROOOOMMMM*
> HoneyB: *OK*
> HoneyB: *::::::brushing your cheek softly with my fingertips::::::*

They're off and running, describing the sights and sounds as imaginatively as they can. Important clues to deeper feelings come with the speed of your partner's typing, word choices, and use of symbols, like the emoticons that we discussed in the last chapter. They will become second nature in your online dialogues. Actions and thoughts are indicated with colons (::::breathing heavily:::::) to separate them from spoken words, and the little smilie on its side :) is extremely useful.

Sometimes very frank discussions take place in public chat rooms. And as we mentioned earlier, these public rooms may be carefully policed on the major online services. If a conversation gets racy, the participants are quickly ushered into a private room or even tossed out of the service for a period of time. On AOL members have a choice when they log on of going into the public rooms (room names created by the sysops) or "member" rooms (room names dreamed up by the members themselves) or creating their own private rooms, as HansomJack did. Typical public rooms might be "Romance Connection" or "Gay and Lesbian Chat." Member rooms might be "Hot f Looking for Hot m," "Reno Roadhouse," or "Byte Me." If you choose a member room, you can expect a more explicit conversation, though they are also policed from time to time. Fantasy and role play abound as words scroll down your screen, and it can be fun to sample one room after another until you find a group that is interesting. Public rooms and member rooms are for meeting others, and private rooms are for getting down to serious playing, without any censorship.

Who is having cybersex and, my goodness, why?

What is the point of this electronic foreplay or cybersex? Some people are sincerely trying to find someone with whom they can form a deeper real-life relationship, some are just enjoying playing with words on the computer, and some are hoping to meet someone for a one-night stand, or an affair, in person. Many have wives or husbands, girlfriends or boyfriends. All seem to be looking for an extracurricular sexual outlet. And computer sex is safe sex and available easily, literally at your fingertips.

Many online chatters are lonely and looking for a way to meet new friends. Those who are looking for something more find this first step, an online conversation, relatively easy. Sometimes letting your imagination go can allow a release of inhibitions. Strangers are able to connect intellectually in a fantastic new way. People who meet online and enjoy a wonderful cybersex adventure may or may not decide to meet each other in person. If they meet, they usually find each other intelligent, attractive, and interesting whether or not a relationship continues in real life. Even though your new friend may not look exactly as you expected, it doesn't seem to matter very much since you know each other in a much deeper way, from the inside out. More often than you might think, people fall truly in love online, meet in real life, and decide to marry. And, if you already have a true love in your life, chatting with your "puter-pals" can be just a fun way to unwind at the end of a day.

THE GAMEBOX

Dream On—Create your own room or forum on your BBS and see who comes in to chat with you. You might name your special room "Naked Truth" or "Mr. Good's Bar." Be lively and creative and keep the conversation flowing...:) If there are more than six people in your room at the end of 30 minutes, you WIN.

Cybersex can be marvelously exciting. A creative fantasy is great fun when the partners are responsive and clever and the imagery good. In the real world, sex involves a special combining of bodies; in the virtual or computer world, sex involves a combining of minds. And it can be very powerful stuff. Now, you probably have a mental picture of two people typing sexy words to each other while masturbating, but this is simply incorrect in most cases.

Since many "unconnected" people think this is what cybersex is all about, let's consider this aspect. Masturbation, or self-pleasuring, is an accepted way to appreciate and know your own body and the pleasurable sensations it can give you. And for some, it heightens the online cybersex experience. But for most, electronic foreplay leads to a richer offline experience. Married people find that an evening spent in front of the computer engaging in an arousing or libidinous dialogue enhances their relationship with each other. Jefferson D. says, "It has improved my real-life relationship 100%. Sex on the computer has led to a much richer sex life with my wife—sort of a jump start."

Is it cheating?

You may have to think about this in terms of your own life, but most onliners don't take playing online seriously. Steve R. tells Delilah, "Being married, you give up some aspects of your nature—sort of like being castrated where other women are concerned. The primal skill of seduction, like the instinct for hunting, is necessary for survival of the species. And my online adventures help me rediscover these skills. When women flirt online they feel beautiful and sexy. Perhaps there will be fewer divorces when more married people discover cybersex."

Kathy T. tells Delilah, "As women enter their 30s and 40s their interest in sex enjoys a renewal. But men's interest hits a plateau. Women have always been taught they are 'bad' if they do anything about these feelings. Cybersex gives them a good way to be 'bad' without the guilt."

Cybersex can mean something different for everyone, but most onliners agree that it seems to enhance real-life sex. "I am happily married with two children," Harrison states. "I am also a public figure in my community. These facts add a certain irony to my computer fun and games and definitely heighten pleasure both online and in real life."

Now back to HoneyB and HansomJack:

HansomJack:	::::::putting my arm around your shoulders:::::
HoneyB:	:::::snuggling closer to you:::::
HoneyB:	It's really beautiful up here!
HansomJack:	::::tilting your face up to mine:::::
HansomJack:	::::kissing you gently:::::
HoneyB:	I'm feeling all warm and mushy :::arms around your neck:::::
HansomJack:	You smell soooo good!
HansomJack:	:::::sliding my warm hand between your legs::::::
HoneyB:	Ooohh
HoneyB:	:::::tasting your lips:::::: Oh, Baby!
HansomJack:	:::::touching your damp panties::::::
HoneyB:	:::::::slipping my tongue into your mouth:::::::::

Well, you get the idea.

The next step for some can be actual phone conversation, often incorporating sex. This has more significance than simple phone sex, which uses a 900 number. If you have been involved in many online dialogues with someone you enjoy and find the scenes creative and stimulating, a phone conversation can make the experience even more pleasurable. If you have a built-in resistance to this idea, or if you feel it is inappropriate, skip it. Trust your instincts and pay attention to cues or warning signals of activities or people that make you uncomfortable. Chatting online should be fun for everyone, whether you get deeply involved in a sexual scenario or just enjoy the game-playing and the challenge of using words to create interesting fantastical experiences.

How can this possibly work?

In recent years, there have been many new theories and discoveries about the brain and what makes people tick. It is thought that the left hemisphere of our brains is responsible for the more practical, analytical part of us and the right hemisphere is responsible for the creative, imaginative part of us. This right side, according to studies, guides our sexual behavior. So it is through the process of creative visualization, centered in the right side of our brains, that we can derive great sexual pleasure. Is it any wonder that cybersex works? Visualization of a great sexual fantasy can seem very real. We can produce, direct, and act out our own sexual scripts. And the advantage of being able to change our sexual scripts is that we don't get bored. We introduce novelty by using our imaginations. And we can explore our sexual inhibitions. We can travel to new and exciting places. You may meet your friends for a virtual weekend camping trip in the Rocky Mountains and never leave your home. The possibilities are endless. Good online communication takes concentration. But with practice you can master this process, this right brain activity, which is necessary for a really great experience online.

Many have said that the mind is the most powerful of all our sex organs. Our sexuality is between our ears and not between our legs. Good concentration means keeping images alive and never boring. And if the conversation gets tedious online, just "poof" (disappear) and find another, more interesting group to play with.

Eric is a master at capturing his lady's attention and establishing a connection. Let's eavesdrop on his conversation as he talks with Eve:

Eric:	*Come lay here beside me on the sweet grass, Eve. I want to whisper to you. (He has created an inviting mental picture and set the stage for a quiet, intimate conversation.)*
Eve:	*:::::moving carefully to your side::::::
Eric:	*:::::::sweeping your silky hair back from your face::::::: I love to look at you. (He makes Eve feel young and pretty.) :::::reaching up to your cheek:::::
Eve:	*I'll bet you say that to all the ladies…*
Eric:	*Actually, I feel an unusual chemistry with you…may I kiss you? (And he is sooooo polite!)*
Eric:	*:::::you feel my warm breath as I lean forward to kiss your pink, swollen lips, my tongue briefly touching them ever so gently::::::::: (Eric has cleverly engaged Eve's senses of sight, smell, touch, and taste. She won't forget him quickly.)*

Delilah believes that women especially benefit from online time-outs. Their days are often filled with pressures both at work and at home, numerous interruptions, and very little time to themselves. But an hour with online friends after work can be wonderfully relaxing. And if that special someone describes a soothing massage, a lovely warm bath, or even a walk along the beach in the setting sun, a woman can make an easy transition from her hectic work world to a quiet and calm evening. Each individual tends to have personal preferences, such as being offered a tall glass of iced tea or just a quiet conversation, that work for them in these delightful online fantasies. Usually, an activity focusing on the senses will be calming and enjoyable. Some pleasant sensual verbs to incorporate might include the following: stroke, lift, clasp, sweep, tickle, pat, graze, press, embrace, fondle, brush, savor, and nibble. In a description, choose adjectives carefully. How about spirited, comely, radiant, noble, virile, or superb? Made-up words or putting two words together can be wonderfully effective as well. How about talktime, smoooooth, handholding, babygirl, mypet, dearman, or loverlass? You want to be noticed online, so try something unusual.

As you may have gathered by now, the most creative online chatters are able to introduce a touch of reality by describing what something smells like or tastes like, etc. An element of surprise can be delightful. This is done by either what is written or the way it is written. For instance:

PatE: ::::::::*sitting down on the bed*::::::::

TommyT: ::::*taking my shirt off*::::::::

TommyT: RRRIIIIIIIIIIIIIPPPPPPPPPPPPPPPPPPP

Writing "rip" that way makes it almost hearable and should bring a smile from PatE. Saving capital letters for emphasis gives them more power: "nooooo," "no," and "NO" all have very different meanings, from "maybe" to "I don't think so" to "Don't ask again!"

In real life, our sense of touch is extremely important. It stimulates and heightens all of our other senses. So if you are trying to describe an effective online situation, bring touch into your description. Licking whipped cream off your fingers after buying a sundae for your date or rubbing your face with a warm towel in a virtual Japanese restaurant can create a very sensual feeling in your online partner. Your senses are being stimulated in a pleasurable way. Great online experiences can result from the careful description of giving someone a bath or back rub. And don't forget about painting toenails or taking a walk together. In short, stop and think about the sensual pleasures you experience each day. Concentrate on what you feel when you wash your hair or smooth oil or lotion on your skin, then put it into words on your computer screen.

As you lead your online friend through a great sensual fantasy, concentrating on sights and the way things feel, don't forget our other senses: smell, hearing, and taste. Describe the wonderful scent of a freshly picked rose on a summer afternoon. Rob R. likes to cook and enjoys describing his beautiful breakfasts: buttermilk biscuits dripping with honey, crispy bacon, and scrambled eggs with fried onions. Can't you smell his fresh ground Colombian coffee? Food is always a winner in an online fantasy.

Our sense of hearing is easily reached through our music. Ask your new friend what music she likes, then stop into your favorite CD store and check out the latest disks. When you next meet online, you can suggest some new music she might like. You might even take her cyber-dancing at the Post Oak Ranch in Houston. The following chat really happened in a room called the Texas Tavern one warm summer night. Even though the names have been changed, you may recognize this group.

BorderTown:	A tip of the hat to all the lovely ladies in the Tavern. Who wants to mosey out onto the dance floor with this ol' cowboy tonight?
Rose o' Texas:	<———-waiting for a cowboy to take a little piece of her heart. I'd love to move with you around the floor... :::::smiling sweetly::::::
LoneRanger:	:::::dropping a couple quarters in the jukebox:::::

Rose o' Texas:	Careful, hon, they just put sawdust on the floor...:)
BorderTown:	Just a little piece of your heart, darlin'? ::::my arm pulls your body next to mine, and both my arms encircle you as we dance::::: How about the whole thing? You are a mighty cute little filly.
TexHeart:	Since I am the barmaid, here's... C(_) [_]... frosty beer and shots all around... ::::sliding the glasses down the bar:::::::
Rose o' Texas:	∿∿"Waltzing Across Texas"∿∿ with tall BorderTown
BorderTown:	You are gonna shine my belt buckle, sweet thang! :::moving in circles gracefully around the floor::::::
PrairieDawg:	Here are silver $$$$$$$$ for the drinks, TexHeart.
TexHeart:	::::opening my blouse to catch the $$$$$$::::: How about a (_) brandy for Hawk? I'm glad your wife let you out tonight!
Hawk:	Me too! And I'd like to buy a drink for Ruby! ::::winking at Ruby::::: What would you like, sweet lady? ::::tipping my cowboy hat:::::::
Ruby:	Thanks Hawk...make it QUERVO gold and a <) lime, please :::::smiling at a mighty cute Hawk:::::

This party will go on for hours, some couples will disappear to the loft for cybersex, and the sheriff will come and try to collect all the guns. There will be at least one bar fight, but we can't stay. You will have to imagine the narrations from 20 people in many different cities all online at once as they describe the sound of the linedancers' boots, frothy margaritas, whirling skirts, and the guitar licks of Junior Brown. All this can create an image so powerful that you might have to stop typing to catch your breath.

Now let's take off our cowboy hats and talk about a serious subject—honesty online. How honest are people you meet in the interactive online service you have chosen? In the beginning, you can't be sure. As we have mentioned, some major services and BBSs allow members to provide a history or profile, but there is really no way to check these facts. However, if you chat for many hours with someone, perhaps over an extended period of time, a true picture can emerge. Is your online friend consistent in what he or she says? Do the stories seem believable? Does the portrait painted seem too perfect to be true? If it does, it probably is! You often have to read between the lines.

The area which we all tend to exaggerate is our physical attributes. Physical attraction is an important part of sexuality. Every culture all over the world has certain standards by which it judges physical beauty. And we all know these standards can be very different from place to place. In American culture, we all strive to look like models and movie stars. And there is a huge temptation to describe ourselves in the best possible light. In a very informal survey of men and women online, the general consensus was that women tend to tell their partners that they are slimmer than they are, and women report that many men make themselves taller and more successful in their business endeavors than they may be. This should not be surprising because we want to impress and we want to pretend that we are more attractive and interesting. But there is a difference between creating a fantasy and being dishonest. If you purposely mislead your computer sweetheart, it may come back to bite you. One medical doctor who met his wife online said that he had to send her a copy of his MD degree to prove to her that he was actually a physician.

After you get used to online conversation, you will begin to understand the erotic power of imagination. The sexy stories we create can seem very real, and the people we play with can become genuine friends. We begin to realize that what is inside—our personality and heart—is more important than our physical characteristics. Some people are more flexible about the physical makeup of their friends, and if we can be flexible, we can look for real depth of character. This is surprisingly easy online. The physical part of someone we have gotten to know is much less important than if he or she is witty, clever, funny, or interesting. Perhaps we admire their extreme intelligence. Maybe we love to laugh at their clever way with words. Or perhaps we enjoy their ability to engage us in a lovely cybersex adventure. Carol Wells tackles the difficult real-life question of whether an initial strong physical attraction is necessary for a rich sexual experience in her book *Right-Brain Sex* where she states that "the more flexible we are, the less important physical beauty is." If you decide to meet your online love, you may find that it doesn't matter very much what he or she looks like. Online communication is breaking down many barriers.

Now let's suppose you have made a wonderful connection online. You have talked for many weeks or months and feel you really know each other, and the date is set for a real-life meeting. There are some cautionary points to keep in mind. Be a bit careful. You should meet in a public place. Many onliners like to meet the first time at a "bash," or special party. These get-togethers are held in hotel suites or restaurants all over the country. And be prepared: perhaps the excitement you felt online won't be there when you meet in person. However, getting to know someone from the inside out should have enabled you to broaden your friendships as well as your attitudes about superficial qualities.

"I would never meet anyone in real life that I have had cybersex with," insists Martin in Los Angeles. "There could only be one of two outcomes. The first is that I would be really disappointed. We tend to see our online friends as larger than life. The second is that I could find my online partner extremely attractive and end up ruining my marriage. It isn't worth that."

THE GAMEBOX

Bashing—Attend a "bash," or party, to meet fellow onliners. Bashes are held as impromptu get-togethers or large, carefully planned, and extravagant gatherings. If you can't locate one in your area, participate in the planning and get a group of cyberfriends together. To find out how to go about putting such an affair together, just ask others online...:) It's easier than you might think.

What do you mean, it can change my life?

Sharon: I have met a wonderful man online. He is divorced also, and we talked for five hours the first night! We have so much in common, and he is coming to visit me next month! I think this is the best possible way to meet someone. You get to know them BEFORE you meet them.

Illinis: Computer chatting is really amazing. I feel like my attitudes have been broadened in so many ways. I enjoy discussing all sorts of things with new friends in several age groups. We would never have met a few years ago.

It's a fact that computers are changing our lives. And, as always with huge changes in technology, critics insist the sky is falling. Those who view computers as a threat to society by depersonalizing our interactions with each other fail to take into account the human spirit. Instead of being isolated in little cubicles, we play together with abandon in a wonderful cyberspace behind our computer screens. You have to experience it to fully appreciate the enchantment. If Robert Jahn, a Princeton University scientist, is correct in his theory that humans can influence machines with their minds, is it so difficult to believe that two people can become mindmates through their computers?

To delve once more into Carol Wells's book, let's look at the idea of just plain having fun. She states that pleasure and play go together. They give us relief from the pressures and trials of our everyday world. And logging onto an online service from your office desk at the close of your day can give you such a dose of fun and pleasure. A single, young attorney in Chicago told Delilah that this is the best part of his day. He checks for special friends just to ask "How are you doing?" He has communicated often with several special young ladies and, although he has yet to meet one in real life, this may be the next step for him. He doesn't drink and finds it much more enjoyable to chat for awhile without the hassle of a bar atmosphere. And he finds his sex life online gives him fun and pleasure, though it is, of course, not a substitute for the real thing. "Almost all the young ladies I have met online tell me they have a 36D bra size. I ask you, just what are the chances of that?" he laughingly remarked.

Keeping a playful outlook is always important in this life. It will keep boredom from your door. And "those of us who know how to truly play, also know how to experience pleasure," states Wells. Learning how to play online and joining that with the pleasure, and perhaps even lust, of cybersex will allow us to "keep investing in life, in spite of difficulties, setbacks, painful losses, or failures."

Terri:	*My kids got me interested in online fun and games...and I think it has brought our whole family together.*
TomT.:	*I have met several ladies online that I think I would really enjoy meeting. I am trying to work up my courage for that!*

The people involved in the following conversation know how to play. In an open forum, Delilah recorded this discussion connecting three threads: sky-diving, sex, and pizza.

SKYWALKR:	I haven't tried sky diving yet.
RonRoy:	Two minutes of free-fall is sort of like sex.
TinyTim:	You mean bad sex or good sex, Ron?
SandraDee:	I never would be that brave—I mean about the free fall...
Whitney:	Hell, the worst sex I ever had was wonderful.
Morningstar:	At least bad sex is better than no sex.
RonRoy:	I jumped out of a plane at 8000 feet, and it was FANTASTIC!!
Whitney:	Sex is like pizza. Even when it's bad it's good.
SKYWALKR:	You'd rather have it than not...like pizza?
SandraDee:	How is skydiving like sex, Ron?
RonRoy:	I enjoy the thrust, soaring from the ground and watching the earth fall away...
RonRoy:	Then when you jump, it's the opposite. You watch the earth come at you quickly.
SKYWALKR:	Ron, that reminds me of when my wife caught me having cybersex on the computer. She came at me quickly!
SandraDee:	LOL (laughing out loud)
Whitney:	Notice what got us all talking...SEX...not a bad topic.
SandraDee:	I thought we were talking about skydiving.
Morningstar:	Nope. We are talking about pizza. Ron, have you ever had sex while skydiving and eating pizza?
Whitney:	Ever dived into a pizza parlor? And had sex with the counter person?
RonRoy:	I have a friend that landed in a shopping center parking lot once...

And so on, and so on, and.... Jump in and see what it's all about. Your new cyber-pals are waiting for you—perhaps in the hot tub.

5

Can We Talk?

:::leading you step-by-step:::

Q. Dear Delilah,
I have heard some wild stories about online relationships. What
problems should I watch out for? And are there REAL dangers?
                                                    LILA in Pittsburgh

A. Dear LILA,
The virtual or online community is like a real-life community. You
DO have to take some precautions, just as you do in Pittsburgh.
But thousands find friendship and fun on their computers without
any difficulty.

This chapter is not meant to discourage you from the
wonderful opportunities in cyberspace, but you should
be aware of the possible "crashes." I do believe that the
good things outweigh the bad. And hopefully, reading
this little guide will help you to discern the hurtful
games-players from the upstanding individuals online.

But sometimes there are surprises: there have even
been numerous citings of wolves online. How can you tell

who is a real wolf? We will take a serious look at this, but first, for some fun, let's look at Brian Y.'s humorous guidelines for determining the difference between wolves and gentlemen:

A computer gentleman sends online flowers, hugs, and kisses.

A computer wolf sends lewd instant messages.

A computer gentleman asks, "Do you and your husband have any children?"

A computer wolf asks, "What time does he leave for work in the morning?"

A computer gentleman has a pleasant name like "Doug" in his screen name.

A computer wolf has the number "69" in his screen name.

A computer gentleman wants to know some tips on dating and relationships.

A computer wolf wants to know your favorite position.

Did you hear the story about...?

"I have never been so humiliated!" These words were said in an open online discussion. Ginny had been talking for weeks, both on her computer and on the phone, to a man who told her he was recently divorced. He said he was the CEO of a large New York based corporation and sent her company documents prominently displaying his name to prove it. He told her he cared deeply for her, called her many times a day to share business concerns, asked her advice, and even gave her his phone numbers. After an exhilarating weekend together at a Connecticut resort, she unexpectedly called his home number, and, to her shock, a surprised feminine voice answered, saying she was his wife. Needless to say, Ginny felt terribly hurt and refused to have any further communication with this man she had trusted.

Stories like this are unfortunate reflections of the darker corners in cyberspace, where the wolves hide. Let's shine some cautionary light into those corners.

Delilah advises: Re-read "Little Red Riding Hood."

What are the dangers?

Many onliners use their computer contacts as social outlets when traveling to other cities on business, and lunches or dinner get-togethers to put faces and screen names together are commonplace. All this can make

business travel much more interesting and lots more fun. But some people are totally dishonest, and an online relationship with them can result in a painful emotional down. It is a sad fact that some married business travelers see their online chums merely as sexual diversions. And it is easy to trust and share online—easier than in our real-life world, where conditioning and layers of socialization afford us protection. The following stories are reminders to be cautious.

Susan tells of an online stalking that frightened and intimidated her. Her online "friend" called her at all hours of the day and night and eventually threatened to meet her when she was picking her children up at their school. In her fear that this could endanger her children, she decided to relocate, at great inconvenience and cost.

Alas, there have even been accounts of rape when unsuspecting women have met their online male friends in quiet, out-of-the-way settings or hotel rooms. Delilah repeats: Always meet in a public place, like a party or bash held especially for onliners to get together. No one wants to see another become a victim in any way, but, as in real life, there are perverted spoilers online as well. We have said this before, but it bears repeating: You should be very careful about revealing your true name, address, and phone number to anyone.

Sometimes the danger online is directed at your wallet. PRETTYLADY happened into an open forum, where computer hackers were busily collecting IDs and passwords from those novice onliners too inexperienced to know better than to give out that information. The cheaters claimed to be online service representatives, and after collecting private information that would allow them access to accounts, log-on time, and even credit card numbers, they promptly poofed. Then the offending few could change their online names, or even cancel their own accounts, thereafter using the identities and credit of others. Situations can develop fast online, and damage can be done with the speed of a keystroke.

If you run into an online cad or suffer a heartbreak, you have three choices: GET HELP (talk to someone who can help you work it through), GET EVEN (report the offender to your sysop or even the police in an extreme case), or GET SMART (don't let it happen again!).

> *Delilah advises:* Never give out personal information in a public forum online, and be extra careful when meeting an online friend in real life.

By now you understand that cyberspace is unlike any place you have ever been before. It is wonderful, exciting, challenging, and sometimes even a bit dangerous. People you meet are at once anonymous and exposed. They can be very friendly, yet mysterious. Conversations seem to be open, honest, and very revealing. And when men and women meet in this uninhibited and exciting new way, it is inevitable that romances blossom. In fact, most onliners who spend much time on the chat boards seem to be in some kind of relationship with a cyberfriend, and these relationships can pose serious problems if they aren't kept in perspective.

What if we're married?

Let's examine what can happen when two people fall in love via their computers. After all, this is a guide to cyberlove. There are many emotional undercurrents online, and simple fun and games that get serious can create problems in real life for those consenting adults at play in cyberspace.

Some say a modem should come with a sort of warning label: CAUTION—PLAYING ONLINE MAY BE DANGEROUS TO YOUR PSYCHE. Computer interaction is great amusement and begins innocently enough. "Tell me what you look like." These words scroll over and over on computer screens everywhere, and the answers can be whatever you want them to be. That is the fun of computer communication. But is there a danger in creating a fantasy persona and having a fantasy love affair? Have onliners found a new way to cheat on each other and on their real-life spouses? Is it really cheating? The answer to these questions is "Perhaps." It all depends on you.

Online stories are as varied as the people chatting. For some, typing sexy thoughts to an anonymous sweetheart can become a risky alternative to working on a real-life relationship, a further distancing of one person from others. Psychologists consider it a sexual disorder when online chat becomes a substitute for a real sexual relationship.

Delilah finds that many married couples do not tell their spouses of their online friendships when one person is more computer-active than the other. "My online sweetie adds a new dimension of excitement to my otherwise rather routine and boring life," states Paul G. "I don't plan to meet her in real life, but we do talk often on the phone, and I really do care for her. However, I don't want to do anything to upset my marriage and family. If I must honestly answer the question of 'why have an online love,' I guess I would answer that this fantasy allows me to explore a sexual relationship with another in a safe way. It makes my real-life sex more stimulating and vibrant. And if my wife doesn't know about it, what is the harm?"

And Jennifer tells Delilah, "My husband finds my computer fun and games amusing. But I agree to stay offline when he is home, in the evenings and on the weekends. I find having a special 'online husband' gives a new dimension to my everyday world. My online friend is a wonderful, caring man, and we can talk about anything. But we will probably never meet each other since we are both happily married in real life. Why ruin a wonderful fantasy?"

Delilah might tell Paul G. and Jennifer that it could even be more fun to share computer games WITH their spouses. Lots of husbands and wives find this online electronic foreplay to be very exhilarating, and they share the following really interactive games:

GAMES

Hide 'n Seek

Harry hides his favorite weekly story from the alt.sex.stories newsgroup on the Internet for Sherry to find—in the pantry, under her pillow...:)

Talk

Sam and Karen log onto their BBS every night together to see how long it will take one of them to engage someone in cyber-sex. They time each other, and Karen is winning.

Musical Chairs

Tom and Judy take turns in the computer seat, each telling the other what to type to their online lovers.

A GIF Is Worth More Than a Thousand Words

Heather downloads an interesting GIF (computer photo) every week for husband Terry. He rates them on a scale of 1–10 and gives her points for lingerie shopping: 10 points = $100.00.

Three-Way Phone Sex

Connie calls her online love Todd on the telephone when she and her real husband make whoopie, so he can join in.

And here's a game you can begin tonight with your real-life sweetie.

THE GAMEBOX

Mystery E-mail—Send sexy E-mail messages to your spouse or real-life love from an anonymous "pen-pal" for several days. If you can get him or her to agree to meet you, you WIN.

Onliners never seem to tire of debating the ethics and morality of cybersex. In a discussion on whether or not engaging in computer sex is being unfaithful to a real-life spouse, Delilah recorded the following comments:

RandyMan: CSex is a situation of computer/brain interface.

JennyO: It depends on what you mean by cheating—is it cheating to flirt?

Chris111:   Online sex is not as much fun—it CAN'T be immoral!

RandyMan: Online activity amounts to no more than fantasy or reading a Playboy, etc.

RaeBo: It is sure "alove" and well…

JennyO: Having Csex under a pseudonym is the equivalent of an electronic condom.

Chris111:   I think it all depends on how stable a married couple's relationship is in the first place…

There are a lot of interpretations afloat about the nature of online relationships, but there is no doubt that finding a love relationship can result in real-life cheating. The participants may move quickly from computer chat to phone conversation, then to a real-life meeting. But if one or both partners is married or truly committed to another, the stage is set for deep hurt, even a devastating situation. And if there are problems within the marriage or relationship—and who doesn't have problems—the danger is compounded.

BruceT's real-life wife called his online service when

she became suspicious of his unusually high telephone charges and asked for specific information from the billing department. She requested his passwords and account numbers and was then able to go into his mail and read messages from his online girlfriend. Needless to say he had a lot of explaining to do. Could it be that, just perhaps, this danger adds to the attraction and titillation of online fun and games? :)

Don and Sara also played with fire. Don had been chatting with Sara every morning from his office terminal before starting his work day as a busy patent attorney. She worked in a similar office only blocks away. He found Sara caring, responsive, and very entertaining. She found him wonderfully witty and clever. They got to know each other very well. After several days of meeting online, it wasn't difficult for them to agree on a lunch date. On the appointed day, Sara found herself taking special care in her dress, hair, and makeup—preparing for a really special date. And Don found he was so excited to meet this sweet mystery woman that he could hardly concentrate on work.

Sara had been married in real life for nine years, and Don had just celebrated his thirteenth wedding anniversary. They told themselves this was a wonderful new "friendship" and harmless fun. Although they loved their spouses, their lives had become routine, even boring, and the sparks flew at their first lunch meeting. They were soon getting together regularly and telling lies to their spouses. When Sara's husband discovered the dalliance, he was naturally furious. He packed his bags and moved to a hotel. Don, in a panic, severed his friendship with Sara, stopped his online activity, and rebuilt his relationship with his wife. Eventually, Sara was able to reconcile with her husband, but this true story gives us an idea of the power of computer communication that allows us to get to know someone in a deeper way than we ever would in casual real-world contact.

SlipNot, an online friend, is fond of this quote from Andy Warhol: "Fantasy love is much better than reality love. Never doing it is very exciting. The most exciting attractions are between two opposites that never meet." And if you channel the excitement of an online love affair to play in real life with your spouse or significant other, you can enjoy a renewed interest in each other. However, if your real-life relationship is shaky or failing, it might have an opposite effect. So be careful. Be up-front with your spouse if you can. Having an online love may not be worth the pain, anguish, and ultimate loss of a real-life love. Or, if you really want out of your marriage, it may be…:)

Delilah advises: Be honest, stay true, and keep the fun in perspective.

By the way, can we do some business?

If you are interested in networking for business, and many are, you can always mention it to the people you are chatting with online. You can also mention your occupation in the information about yourself that you provide for your online service directory. The Internet can bring people with common interests together, and business contacts often develop into deep friendships, as the following story about Tammy and Stan illustrates.

Tammy T. owned a small flower business in California. She decided to advertise on the World Wide Web after watching her business grow through a carefully placed ad on CompuServe. Stan P., a rose grower in Colorado, noticed her clever Valentines' Day promotion on the Web and contacted her to see if they could do some business together. After months of conversation online and several business transactions, they decided to meet each other in Denver. They had already shared much about themselves, about their personal lives as well as business goals, and were delighted to finally meet. Both were single and looking for a more meaningful relationship in their lives, and they felt they might have found that in each other. In an E-mail to Delilah, Tammy mentioned that she was even thinking of relocating to Colorado! They would probably not have met if it weren't for the far-reaching highways on the Internet.

We wish Tammy and Stan the best of luck, but if you are thinking of entering into a business relationship with your new online friend, be cautious until you get to know this new friend well—that is, in the real world. Business opportunities can be fantastic but also risky.

> *Delilah advises:* Always get professional advice before entering into any business arrangement.

Help! I'm addicted! (Delilah's 12-step program)

Is there such a thing as an addiction to computer communication? Again, the answer is "Yes." Many people get hooked. Onliners speak in jest about a 12-step program to curtail their time spent online. Jeffery 246 said on Prodigy that he believes in a direct approach: "unplug the damn computer." And in the March 1995 issue of *Computer Life*,* Gregg Keizer listed several tongue-in-cheek symptoms of computer addiction. You're in trouble when:

> During a 2 a.m. call to the bathroom you check your e-mail.
>
> Your neighbor mentions taking a drive, you think not miles but megs.

*Reprinted from "Computer Life," March 1995, Copyright © 1995 Ziff-Davis Publishing Company L.P.

Down at the local computer store they know your name and
favorite chip.

You have chronic lower back pain, knots in your shoulders, and a
cramp in your mouse finger, and you can't see more than
three feet in front of your face. (This rings Delilah's bell.)

Your penmanship looks worse than it did in the fourth grade.

You don't throw out bad floppies, you decorate them and use
them as drink coasters.

Delilah has come up with her own 12-step program to
curb this addiction/compulsion before it gets out of
hand:

1. Admit to yourself that you have a problem.

2. Admit to someone else that you have a problem.

3. Stay offline for three days to condition yourself.

4. Wear mittens after 5:00 p.m.

5. Choose *GQ* at the magazine rack instead of
   Boardwatch.

6. Drive BY Computer City.

7. Stop talking as if Windy1 and DallasDarlin live next
   door.

8. Take a walk instead of "surfing" the Net.

9. Buy a health club membership instead of a new
   hard drive.

10. Set an oven-timer to monitor your online time.
    (Two hours a day is recommended...:)

11. Pay attention to the oven-timer.

12. Go back to step 1 and start over.

On the more serious side, a Harvard Medical School

addictions expert reports that "a certain segment of the population can develop addictive behavior—a sort of cocaine-like rush—in response to online stimulation. It is not as reliable as cocaine or alcohol, but in the contemporary world, it is a fairly reliable way of shifting consciousness." You know you are addicted when you plan your whole day around your computer time and begin to feel your online friends are more real than the people you see each day. And if you are thinking of buying a laptop with a built-in modem so you can stay in touch with your new friends at all hours, everywhere you go, you are in trouble.

Many people simply say good-bye when they find they are spending too much time and money online and cancel their memberships. These tearful farewells are quite commonplace.

Tabby:	*This is it, friendlies. This is my last day on Prodigy. I will miss you all so very much.*
LIINDAA:	*Ohhh, Tabby. We will miss you too. How come you are leaving us?*
Tabby:	*I need to get my life back. Things are falling apart at home, and I know I am not concentrating on my work either. I have spent too much time here.*
LIINDAA:	*This is a sad day. But we will look for you in the future. Perhaps a few months away will help. And I have heard it's best to stop cold turkey…:(* *{{{{{{{{{{{{hugs}}}}}}}}}}}} and* ***************kisses!*

Delilah advises: Never let your online service bill exceed $400.00 monthly…:)

(Delilah is delighted to report that Tabby was recently spotted on a freenet BBS out of Buffalo, New York!)

6

What Are the Men Saying?

::: uploading good pick-up lines :::

Q. Dear Delilah,
Don't you think BOTH men and women enjoy talking about sex online?

Wonderin'

A. Dear Wonderin',
Yep, but women have other interests too . . . :)

In *The Literary Companion to Sex,* Fiona Pitt-Kethley states: "The proper study of man is his groin. All history, all wars, religion, art, philosophy, science have been directed at one thing." Perhaps this is a bit overstated, but if the men scream that they are getting an unfair rap concerning their one-track minds online, they should log on using a female screen name and see what happens. Jim Coates, computer writer for the *Chicago Tribune,* signed onto America Online as Miss Ellie and immediately got a message from someone using the screen name

"LUYD." "I asked the sender what LUYD meant," Jim said, "and he told me it meant 'Looking up your dress.' "

Admittedly there are more men online than women, so you won't get a woman's attention for more than a milli-bit with that approach. It's almost as if some of the men online looking for "hot chat" have taken a step back in evolution and want to drag a woman back to the cave by her hair. They are so anxious to get to the sexy stuff, they can't waste typetime being polite. They would never approach a woman in real life like this. It's no wonder that women have set up special forums—even BBSs—for women only. And in the next chapter we will explore some of these.

It's not that women are THAT particular—heck, we want to play too. And as Gerard Van Der Leun writes in *Time* magazine, "Women willing to engage in erotic give-and-take on the networks...are becoming much more prevalent as the medium expands." So here are some tips, guys, to improve your online scoring...:)

Whatcha wearing?

This question can work as a lead into something more and usually comes early in a dialogue between 'puter pals. The answer can set the stage for either a frivolous conversation or something more serious.

"I'm wearing my carefully starched white nurse's uni-form...just got home from work. I suppose you want a back rub...??????" If you want to chat with this woman, she would probably respond best to a serious remark.

"I'm wearing black silk thigh highs...Chanel #5..." A clever and experienced onliner can have his way with this woman; she sounds ready to play. The next step would be for the man to lead her into a conversation about herself, and carefully phrased questions will tell her lots about him as well. A dialogue might go something like this:

> "Didja just get home from work? You must have an interesting job!"

> "I'm a bunny at our local Playboy Club here in the windy city," she quickly types.

> "No kidding," he says. "I haven't been in a Playboy Club for years. Have they changed?"

> "Sure, there is a computer at every table so the members can play, while they *play*."

> "Sounds like a terrific idea to me! BTW, what's your real name, or should I just call you Honey Bunny?"

If they can find some common ground and the chemistry is there, they could end up chatting for hours. Time—and $—definitely fly when you are having fun online. If you are both on CompuServe or America Online, you might ask your new sweetie to step into a private room to act out a wonderful fantasy together.

> "My real name is Heather. What's yours?"

> He quickly types, "My friends call me Nick. And I would love to talk to you more—about your work. Would you come with me to a private room? Let's call it 'Playboy.' "

"LOL"

If Nick keeps Heather's interest, they might decide to take a pretend walk along the beach or make a future date to go pretend gambling in Las Vegas or even on a tour through cyberspace—stopping to carve their initials on a newsgroup "tree" on the Internet. The following might give you some ideas for your next cyberdate.

How Do I Love Thee? Let Me Count the Ways:

1. On a couch
2. In a chair
3. On the floor
4. In a bed
5. In an old car
6. In a new car
7. In a convertible
8. In the front seat
9. In the back seat
10. On the highway
11. Near the airport
12. In a truck
13. In a hayloft
14. In a shower
15. In a Jacuzzi
16. In a boathouse
17. In the woods
18. By a lake
19. On the beach

20. In the mountains

21. On a table

22. In a cafe

23. Under the table

24. ON THE COMPUTER!

25. Still counting…:))

THE GAMEBOX

Your scenario—Dream up your own date scenario and ask someone online to participate. If it takes you less than 10 minutes to get a date, you WIN.

When you set up that next date, be sure you follow through, guys. Don't stand up your online friends. You wouldn't do that in real life, and you shouldn't do it online. Feelings get somehow magnified in computer communication. If Nick misses the next chat-time with Heather, this could happen:

"Heather, I'm so sorrrry! I couldn't get online last night."

"YRS. I thought I saw you in the Wolf's Den about midnight. You going to deny that?" pouts Heather.

"Well, I got on, finally, but it was so late, I didn't think you would wait."

"Hmmmmmmm…sounds like you are way too busy to spend time with little ol' me. Bye, Nick."

Nick probably won't get the chance to make this up. Remember to leave E-mail notes, guys—something special—every day if you want to win her heart. A cute note might have saved Nick from this situation:

Dear HoneyBunny,

I was late for our date, can't find you now. Hope you will E-mail me the minute you get this. I am waiting here for you, with champagne—and a rose in my mouth! @——} ——} ——

Love, Nick

Ladies, you must read between the lines that men write. When they say they are "late," they may mean that they have been detained by another online friend. And when they say they are "separated" from their wives—they may mean since breakfast. You will have to be interesting to talk to if you want get their attention. Don't challenge them or ask where they have been. That will remind them of the possessive women in their real lives. And when they try to be romantic with flowers and wine, compliment them on their clever and fanciful imaginations.

Dear Nick,

Honey, you DO know what I like! I am here and dear for you.

Your Bunny

Want to talk about sex?

As we have said several times, we KNOW this is where most of the guys are heading, but asking this question is probably not the best way to get there. Even the women who are also looking for a sexy chat prefer something a bit more clever.

"What is a sweet girl like you doing in a room like this?" might tickle her fancy.

"Have we met before? Wanna chat for a few minutes— if you're not busy."

Once you have her attention, and she is willing to play, then let the game begin. Or should we say, it begins as a game...

The following is a tongue-in-cheek look at this popular online game:

THE GAMEBOX

The object of the game is to find other people, usually of the opposite sex, get to know them through computer dialogue, and convince them to have sex in words written from your computer to theirs.

Points—As you move through the game, points are accumulated. For instance, getting a person to give you his real name is worth 10 points. A real phone number can net you another 10 points. And a picture sent can gain the receiver 20 points. The ultimate hoped-for meeting is worth 50 points, whether or not real-time sex comes into play. The person accumulating the most points wins.

Hints—Choose an interesting name for yourself. Everyone has a code name, such as TallPaul or PartiPati. These names can be important to that first dialogue. Then create an enticing profile. You can be creative here, but the secret is to mix a bit of truth into your background. If you say you are from Denver, you should know a lot about Denver.

In actuality, online relationships are about much more than accumulating points. If a woman decides her online friend is taking a dalliance much more seriously than she is and wants to end this direction of activity, she should carefully explain her feelings, give him a way to save face, and change course. She might say:

"Sweetheart, I am feeling very confused by all this and need to back off. You are very special and I have enjoyed chatting with you, but I'm just not ready for anything more. It's not your fault."

What do you look like?

This question is usually asked in an attempt to move a lovely fantasy toward reality. Having a mental picture of your cyberpartner can make the fantasy more exciting. And if you are just playing online, a fantasy answer is usually best.

"I'm tall and slim...used to model in my younger days. And I still work out, keep in shape." She sounds great, doesn't she?

"My hair is blonde, my eyes are blue, and I hope you like your ladies curvy." She sounds dreamy.

And you men might say, "I am 6'2", 180 pounds—a lean machine—warm brown eyes but a touch of gray at my temples I must admit." Yummmmmm.

If you are interested in meeting someone in real life, exchanging pictures will probably be a next step, so tell the truth now. "Most of the ladies I met in real life after getting to know them on the computer were on the heavy side," stated MARKSTONE on Prodigy. "It wouldn't have been so bad, if they had been honest about that in the first place." Delilah is telling the truth when she says that after you get to know someone online, looks just don't matter as much. You know about the inner beauty of your new sweetheart. Encourage your lady friend to relax a bit about her looks. And if you need to tone up, GET THEE TO THE GYM! Many have found motivation to get in shape after finding an online love.

Does your husband know you're here?

Men who ask this question sometimes don't want to know the answer. In fantasyland we can be as young or as good looking or as unattached as we want. And this is part of the fun. But if you form a friendship with someone and really get to know that person, you may just find yourself falling in cyberlove. And it is as deliciously exciting as the first time you really fell in love. If both partners are available, they may begin to speak of actually meeting one another. However, if either is married—a common scenario it seems—some caution is needed. As we have said before, cyberlove can evolve beyond cybersex into a really lovely friendship that can last for years, if there is honesty in the beginning. And an online relationship CAN even be healthy for people who are happily married to others if it is kept in the proper perspective—online and not infringing on the marriage. Married couples should be careful about sharing their online activities with a spouse. It doesn't have to be an alarming announcement. "Guess what happened to me online last night?" might introduce the subject in a lighthearted manner. However, whenever you play with emotions, yours or someone else's, you play with fire, so be careful.

The following letter was sent to Delilah by an online friend—a man's point of view:

Dear Delilah,

You may pass this on to your readers...perhaps it will help them. I think the following sentence should be stamped on every modem.

WARNING—This modem can be dangerous to your marriage!

It started simply, the way many major events in life do. I bought an IBM personal computer so my wife could write. She enrolled in a writing class, eager to try her hand at poetry. I have read that often in our middle years, with children on their own, we may consider a new career path. But not in my wildest moments of fantasy would I have anticipated this.

Using the built-in modem, it was a simple task to sign up with an online communication service. Soon, my dear wife, Betty, was chatting away with people all over the country. I often joined her at the computer in the evening. We would click into a "room" to talk with others about the daily news, or perhaps join a group of writers to chat about their ongoing projects. One evening Betty was asked by a man calling himself LoveU2 to join him in a *private* room. Eager to experience everything, she happily agreed, and in 20 minutes they were deeply involved in compusex. He led her on a journey with words—a journey to explore her sexual side. LoveU2 described holding, kissing, and slowly undressing my wife and having sex with her, in front of me. I must admit, we were both surprised and titillated by this new pastime.

This was the beginning, and I really had no warning. Next, Betty became friends with a man in Colorado, whose screen name was DenverDan. They were soon chatting for hours and having compusex without me. He was also an aspiring writer, and they decided to co-write short romantic poems. She would start a poem, upload it to Dan, and he would finish it, then send it back. Sometimes they each added parts, and Dan usually had the job of supplying the erotic phrases. But Bouncin'Betty was a quick study and soon learned to write "sex" herself.

By this time, warning bells were going off. Betty was spending at least 3 hours a day on her poems. I couldn't imagine why Dan had so much time on his hands, but Betty told me that he was writing at odd moments from work—a software programmer seems to have lots of "odd" moments. In fact, my sweet wife knew all about this man and his family. After 235 hours and $349 worth of conversation, she knew so much about him (and he knew as much about us?) that he was beginning to repeat his stories.

I wasn't totally passive for 235 hours. But what could I do? If I said "Stop," she would feel forever thwarted as a successful poet. So I chose to rage inside and trust that this new "friendship" would run its course. However, I misjudged the resolve of this character from the mile high city. He wanted my Betty.

As time went by, the soup thickened. All the ingredients finally boiled to the top when Betty and Dan decided they had to actually meet each other to discuss their upcoming book. My warnings, then rantings, were all unheeded.

On the day Betty was to fly to Denver, I thought there would surely be a last minute reprieve. I hoped she would change her mind—hoped, I'll admit, that Dan himself would call and tell her it wasn't to be. But no. I put her on the plane, my hands stuffed deep into my pockets and a scowl of displeasure on my face. And as I watched her silver 747 lift off into the unusually blue sky over Chicago, I thought seriously of cleaning house—of throwing the computer into the trash.

The next three days I buried myself in work—pushed my anxiety into a closet—trusted that my level-headed wife would return to me less enamored with her new career. We spoke on the phone nightly, and she said they were getting a lot done. She seemed animated and far too happy to suit me.

On the day of her return, a light dusting of snow cleaned her path as she came out to my waiting car. I jumped out to help her and took her eagerly into my arms. To my immense relief, she seemed genuinely happy to see me, and on the drive home she spoke little of DenverDan except in funny anecdotes and stories about her adventure.

As the weeks passed she "talked" on the computer less and less, using it mainly to do basic word processing. She said she had given up on poetry and had started a novel. Hooray! I never asked her what had happened between them. Whatever had gone on before seemed over. She was loving, sweet, and content to be home. Our lives were back to normal! YRS (Yeah! Right! Sure!)

"Not again," I groaned, when she announced that a new agent she had found online was coming to visit her. He said he had to meet with her regularly. I didn't think I could stand being married to a "connected" writer. But that was several books ago—I have adjusted and we have survived.

Now I am the one chatting on the 'puter to sweet things all over the world…:)

But my screen name is OldrNWisr.

Sincerely, Ed

It is a fact that there is a darker side to online activity, and marriages have actually been broken because of an online flirtation. We imagine that another partner might be more interesting or more fun or more caring. Online, we see only a small part of the total person. We don't have to fuss about money or the kids or any of the little problems we all have. But Delilah has heard many stories and concludes that even if two online lovers succumb to a brief affair in real life, they usually return to their actual mates if their marriage is savable—perhaps, as Ed, older and wiser. One more time, keep it all in perspective. Some kind "time-outs" might be:

DimpledDav: *I have enjoyed our chats here more than you know...but it is time for me to focus on my work. I'll keep in touch...*

JRW: *My wife is starting to burn my dinners...LOL. I'm going to give my computer a rest, but have enjoyed talking to you immensely. Take care of yourself.*

PaulieT: *You are a sweet and special lady and deserve to find a man who can give you a secure relationship. ::::::::::stepping out of your way::::::::: Best wishes! I'll never forget our wonderful talks here.*

If things get out of hand, stay offline for a few weeks to regain your distance. Or talk to someone about your concerns. There are plenty of conferences and forums online where you can talk to others who have experienced what you are going through, and they will be happy to share their feelings with you. They may be, in fact, the ONLY ones who will understand.

Can you meet me at the airport?

If you get to this point in your online relationship, there is no turning back. And there is no middle ground. Your online relationship (and your real-world relationships?) may never be the same. By this time you have shared and shared—hours of chatting, pictures, telephone time, maybe even gifts and tapes of music. If you have been honest and your online sweetheart has been honest, there should be few surprises. BUT now you will pass "go" and begin to know each other all over again, with all the advantages of body language, voice nuance, and even real touching. Joe met Christine after months of computer time, only to be ultimately disappointed. Joe tells us:

"At first it was wonderful, and she even moved her real estate license from KS to CA so we could be near each other. But after 6 months both of us were ready to call it quits. She was so absorbed in her kids and their activities, there seemed to be no room for me in her life after all."

Tom M., by contrast, knew immediately that his first f2f with Sandy was the beginning of his new life. "I am very shy, and if I hadn't gotten to know her so well within the safety of cyberspace, we could never have become close. She helped me to open up and we hope to be married next Christmas."

And Roy M. confided to Delilah that he has several friends in three different cities he frequents for business. "We get together for evenings of dinner, dancing, shows, and socializing whenever I am in town. I'm not married and don't want to be. And they understand this—feel the same. We all use the computer to meet other people; then, if the feelings are right, we get together and go from there. It's like a dating service, only better."

If a casual friendship is what you're looking for, these lines might help:

HaroldR: *I'm going to be in your city for several days next week...any chance you might like to have lunch? I'd love to continue our discussion...*

SmilNSam: *My friends have invited me for a golf outing next month near your town. Would you like to get together for coffee? I would love to meet you.*

TerryL: *I managed to find a copy of that book/CD/picture I was telling you about. Any chance I could put it into your sweet hands in person?*

Most onliners agree that the real challenge is moving a computer friendship into a real-life relationship. But more and more people are learning to do this every day, and for many it is a wonderful experience. Guys, we hope these tips will help you!

7

What Are the Women Saying?

::: pouring a cup of coffee ((_)o) for you :::

Q. Dear Delilah,
Where is the FUN I have read about in cyberspace? I want to try
EVERYTHING, but will I be intimidated by all the MEN online?
Andrea in CA

A. Dear Andrea,
It's easy to find the FUN, and you don't sound like the type to be
easily intimidated. When you know where the ON button is, you
also know where the OFF button is, yaknow.

You don't need to know much more than how to turn
your computer on to get connected to all the fun and
games in cyberspace. Studies are finding that more and
more women are learning ALL about their computers.
And they are enjoying it! EDK Associates in New York did
a study showing that as many women as men use computers at work. And after learning about them at work, they
want to use them at home as well. In fact, almost 75% of
all jobs now require some computer skills. So it is no won-

der that the disparity between men and women online is disappearing. Many screen names are nongender-specific, which makes it hard to tell who is male and who is female. But in the public chat rooms of America Online there seems to be an even number of men and women at any given time. Maybell even stopped the chat for 10 seconds with her answer to SUPRMAN.

> "Whatcha driving, Maybell?" asked SUPRMAN.
>
> "Just a little sporty job," answered Maybell. "It's a new Pentium 90 with 2 gig hard drive, 32 megs of turbo charged RAM, a 17-in, 24 bit color monitor, 6x CD-ROM drive, 28.8 superdata highway modem...WHOOOSHHHH...wanna ride?"

I LOVE tall men. How tall are you?

When a woman asks this, she is opening the door for an

interesting scenario that may even include a fantastical adventure with a willing partner clever enough to keep the words new and entertaining. And it will take more than just sexy dialogue.

Some women like to play the field, making no commitments and no attachments. And some would rather build a monogamous relationship over weeks or even months. But in either case, a woman's cyberpartner should be patient and take some time to get to know her. He should be polite, set an interesting stage for the game, and type quickly and cleverly. An experienced online Don Juan is able to read between the lines and understand her moods and wishes by the tone of her typing. RedEagle understands this.

RedEagle: Hi big city lady.

SamanthaT: Hi yourself.

RedEagle: You big city gals don't know what you're missing...

SamanthaT: Really? Where are you?

RedEagle: Texas

SamanthaT: There are big cities in Texas...

RedEagle: But I am not in a city—looking out my window now at a pasture where bluebonnets cover the ground like a carpet. Indian paint brush adds beautiful pale red, blended in with the blue. Ever see something like that?

SamanthaT: Sounds beautiful! Are you a rancher?

RedEagle: Yes, I am. A real cowboy...:) I raise horses and cattle. The air is crisp and clean here, no smoke or smog.

SamanthaT: What are you wearing right now?

RedEagle: A cowboy always dresses from the top down...black cowboy hat, blue long-sleeved shirt, black vest, Wranglers, western belt, and my best Lucchese cowboy boots.

SamanthaT: Hmmmm...you sound lovely. Are you tall too?

> RedEagle: *Yes, ma'am. I am 6'6" in my boots. I am a big man—weigh 260 pounds and it's all muscle. Tell me, have you ever made love in the grass with the scent of crushed flowers floating in the air, and big blue sky overhead...wrapped in each other's arms, feeling no inhibitions, only pure joy at being alive?*
>
> SamanthaT: *Whewwww...what a lovely idea...*

Samantha is drawn into this lovely scene, and as the words scroll down her monitor she can imagine herself in a new place, even as a totally different woman—wild and free, perhaps younger and ravishingly beautiful. She enjoys being romanced, and this is better than reading the latest bestseller because she is actively involved. An interactive story can be enchanting.

You have a wonderful way with words. Are you a writer?

A question like this is the ultimate compliment in computer communication. Online all we have is words, and learning how to put them together is the secret to keeping your new friend's interest. RedEagle has captured her imagination, painted a picture, and now she will want to know more about this sexy new 'puter pal. He is reaching into her mind, so she encourages him with questions and shows her delight in his careful answers.

> SamanthaT: *I think computer sex is fine, but I have to care about someone first...don't you?*
>
> RedEagle: *Sure do. But sometimes people find each other here, enjoy sharing something very special, then go from there....And I feel drawn to you for some reason. Long-legged, big city ladies sure do turn me on.*
>
> SamanthaT: *Describe the room you are in right now...*

RedEagle: I am in my office. It's in my barn overlooking my horse stalls. That way I can talk to you and keep one eye on my stallion down below. He is nervous today...in love I think.

SamanthaT: Do you have a hay loft too?

RedEagle: Of course. It's above my office. And I would love to grab you and hold you tight...carry you up to my hay loft...pitch whoopie.

SamanthaT: But what if I am too heavy for you?

RedEagle: Darlin' I can easily carry two 100 pound feed bags— one on each shoulder. Think you would be too heavy for this cowboy?

SamanthaT: :::::::looking into Eagle's brown eyes::::::::: You could easily lift my 125 pounds then.

RedEagle: :::::::picking you up and starting up the stairs to the loft:::::::

SamanthaT: Ohhhhhh...you are very strong and very solid. I do like that in a man.

RedEagle: Honey, I am indeed a strong man. And I think we would fit together very well. :::::::kissing your neck as I head up the stairs::::::::: I love the way you smell. What perfume are you wearing?

SamanthaT: I am wearing "Poison." You'd better be careful...:)

RedEagle: :::::::laying you down gently in the sweet smelling hay:::::::: I ain't afraid.

SamanthaT: Aren't you gonna take off your hat?

RedEagle: Nope. I never take my hat off during the day...:) A cowboy undresses from the bottom up... :::::::pulling off my cowboy boots:::::::::

SamanthaT: Ohhhhh baby...comere...

With all this chatting going on, you might guess the ladies have discovered a secret. They have found out the REAL benefit to online romance. "The best way to take off five years, and several pounds, at least, is to fall in love every day," insists Margaret R. "Men have been doing this to make themselves feel good for years, and now, thanks to modern technology, women are doing it also. And these mind games don't have to interfere with your real-life marriage or boyfriend; they can be totally risk-free."

Thousands of women log onto their favorite online communication bulletin boards to play and chat before work, at lunch time, after work, and late into the night in their homes across the country. They are finding that having a "boyfriend" makes them care about how they look even if they never meet their online sweetheart. "I haven't had so much fun since I won the local lottery," states Helen, the middle-aged wife of a neurosurgeon in Florida. And come to think of it, it's not unlike the lottery! You don't really know who you are talking to or where they are located—the farther, the better! "When you 'click' with that special someone, it can be wonderfully powerful," laughs Helen.

Anna in California has a glow and bounce to her step that makes her husband rush home every night. He knows she is more responsive and loving than she has been in years. But he doesn't know that this morning she met RobRoy6 on her computer and traveled with him around the world. Rob tells her she is beautiful. He laughs at her jokes and holds her hand. And next week she may sail with Enrico, a wealthy foreign entrepreneur, in a fabulous yacht to a Caribbean island. She may be wined and dined and asked to dance under the stars. And she doesn't even need to leave her house!

The boring and tedious routines of our lives can be eliminated completely. And women all over the country are discovering that by indulging in these little mental time-outs, their eyes are brighter, they stand taller, and those little worry lines around their eyes disappear altogether.

However, a word to the wise: Don't get so caught up in your new hobby that you forget to take the dog out or pick up the children at the sitter's. And don't take your money out of the savings account to fly off with Enrico for a rendezvous on the beach. Remember, to play the online game for these special rewards you must keep it in perspective—the men do. Don't agree to talk on the phone to your new lover or give him your address unless you are willing to risk losing the fantasy. And this rejuvenation comes from the fantasy.

Give it a try. Boot up and log on. Sandra, on Prodigy for three years, insists that she can find exciting romance in not more than 20 minutes any time of the day or night. Granted, not all the men she talks to are clever or quick enough to attract her more than once. But, hey! She is slipping into those tight-fitting jeans with an ease she never expected again! Sandra shared the following with us:

SandraM: *Hey, big guy...what's cookin? (She shows her friend that she has a playful attitude and opens the door for a clever comment from him.)*

SandraM: *I need someone to cheer me up tonight...(She shows her vulnerability with this comment and invites some playtime.)*

SandraM: *You look like someone who would like to have some fun...right?*

(Remember, you can be as forward as you feel like online, ladies.)

Stefanie, an experienced onliner, also believes that most women chatting online are hoping to find that one special cyberfriend to play with, whether or not they are hoping for a real-life romance. She reminds us that flirting online is like flirting in the real world.

"Be a little mysterious—interactive and adaptive. Don't talk too much about yourself. Make a man feel special, and don't be too easy. Make him wonder if you have other online boyfriends, too. Online flirting is safe because it's physically disengaged and anonymous. Keep it that way." Some of Stefanie's favorite lines are:

"*Describe your dream lover for me.*"

"*What excites you most online?*

"*If I were there with you right now, what would you do?*"

"*If you were going to dress me, what would I wear?*"

"*What do you wear to bed at night?*"

If Stefanie has found someone special and wants to get him into a private chat, she might say:

"*Would you like to 'take a walk' with me—in the moonlight?*"

"*Can I sit verrrry close to you?*"

::::::wrapping long arms around your neck::::::

:::::crawling up on your nice lap::::::

When Stefanie is feeling particularly wild, she might use the following lines:

"*If I told you I have been very naughty, would you spank me?*"

"*What would you think if I told you I am bisexual?*"

"*Have you ever engaged in group sex?*"

"*My husband tells me he wants to watch me with another man...whatcha think?*"

"*Do you really get excited when you have computer sex?*"

And if things get wilder than you want, you can use these lines, which Greta L. shares:

"*I am feeling a bit uncomfortable with all this...why do you suppose that is?*"

"*Do you talk to all women this way?*"

"*Oh-oh...phone...bye!*"

JaneJ tells us what NOT to say: (If you use these lines you shouldn't be online!)

"I think all men are pigs."

"You another married cheater?"

"Computer sex is only for people who have NO life."

For the women having a good time, this game works:

THE GAMEBOX

Ladies' Choice—Find a sweetheart online and ask him out for ice cream. Use only one spoon...and describe the "date" in detail. Be inventive and original...:)

It may take some time to become experienced in controlling the online action, and often women are so surprised at the raucous come-ons they don't know how to respond. Let's consider this problem.

Are you serious? Will I do what?

There is a thin but definite line between a titillating dialogue and rude smut, and most women are not interested in engaging in a crude graphic interchange that can make them feel degraded and demeaned. Unfortunately, some men don't understand the difference. They subscribe to the Woody Allen school of thought: when asked if sex is dirty, Woody said, "When you do it right, it is." He was, no doubt, making a joke, but many online lotharios like to try their hands at pornography. Perhaps they have just graduated from graffiti on the school bathroom wall to graffiti on their computer screens. Let's look at the difference between a crude remark and a seductive one.

"I like my women NEKID!" A remark like this made to a

woman new to online chat is not going to be very titillating to her. Everyone knows that wearing a few garments can be more interesting than wearing nothing at all. Sometimes men need to be directed, and a woman might respond, "Well, I'm wearing my new black silk, lacy underthings and a garter belt. Howzat?"

If you want to explore the alternative sexual groups online, it gets particularly dicey. In a domination/submission forum, a woman was asked to submit to being shaved in front of the whole group and to describe her thoughts. Being humiliated is different from being degraded, and she should be led carefully into such a scenario.

"Let's slip you into these little fur-lined handcuffs, darlin'. " (A playful tone helps.)

"I promise you that if you say our "safe" word, I will stop immediately." (Trust has to be established in the very beginning, and 'safe' words to stop the action in D/s games are important.)

The online world is the safest place to explore alternative life-styles. Becky and Phyllis decided to explore their curiosities and began with this discussion:

Becky:	Does the idea of playing with another woman do anything for you?
Phyllis:	You know, I have always wondered about that...
Becky:	In what way? Have you ever tried it? Do you enjoy watching that kind of movie?
Phyllis:	As a matter of fact, I DO enjoy that.

Remember to be creative. Participating in an erotic story is more fun for a woman AND a man. If a man says, "Let's hot chat," a woman might respond, "Let's pretend our eyes have just met on a crowded bus, and something electric jolts us both." However, if he still doesn't get it, she might throw up her hands and look at some of the other interesting activities online. Fortunately there is much online having nothing to do with sex to interest the women. So let's change gears.

Where can I talk to other women?

It is true that for many years men have been the predominant users of personal computers. But even computer companies are aware of the change. At Digital Equipment, engineers are studying the weight of their machines and how difficult it will be for women to pull them out of the box. Suddenly, women are a target for the computer industry, and computer advertising reflects this. Gateway Computers often uses women in their magazine advertisements. One ad shows a woman happily engaged with her laptop computer, a large heart over her head, while her male companion dozes in his lounge chair by her side.

Women are becoming the masters at the communication game. They are not all offended by an instant message that says, "What do you look like?" In fact, women can play the game as well as men. Not only do they enjoy chatting with men via modem, they want to share ideas with other women on sensitive issues such as breast cancer or abortion in special forums or on BBSs that offer a place to discuss women's issues. Some women talk online when no friend is around to take a phone call, and some use their local online service for emotional support. The Over 40 room on America Online is full of chatters who've become good friends, sending messages of encouragement when one is ill or stressed over the ups and downs of life.

From a female point of view, online communication offers an equality found nowhere else. Women are discovering this equality and signing up in record numbers, and they are finding out they have incredible clout. They are definitely in demand in this still primarily male world, and their views are listened to. They can be as outspoken and lusty as they wish.

ECHO, a popular New York BBS, is particularly user-friendly to women, and Stacy Horn, the ECHO president, says there are differences between the ways men and women chat online. "Women tell stories, something personal and all very engaging. Men tell. They like to instruct. They love to answer questions. Their style is less interactive. Women tend to lurk more (read rather than write)." Horn says there is an ECHO rule against personal abuse or harassment. And since women tend to have dominant right brains, where emotions rule, most would rather settle into an interesting forum to share ideas or an interesting sexual fantasy than sit down to play poker on an online casino.

There are BBSs that focus on every hobby you can imagine. Are you interested in jewelry? You might want to try Treasures BBS, located in Longwood, Florida. They began as an E-mail base for importers and wholesalers of Italian gold chains and other fine jewelry and have many representatives online to talk to. They also offer some great games. Are you interested in genealogy? Hall of Records BBS in Hendersonville, North Carolina, is a friendly place to discuss and exchange genealogical information. It was created for those interested in uploading or downloading files in search of information throughout the world. And many professional women are signing onto The Data Highway BBS in Ft. Lauderdale for chat about real estate and investments or to play games such as bridge, backgammon, and Galactic Empire. The sysop Cinda Goodale said, "This is the future of BBSs—real-time discussions, transactions, and interaction worldwide." Pop into your local bookstore and pick up a copy of BBS magazine for information on the latest BBSs and try something new.

Where's the cybermall?

Where are the women who aren't chatting or exploring the newsgroups or working on the family tree? They're shopping!

In the beginning there was the Internet. Most of the techies and geeks (a term of respect these days!) who populated cyberspace in the early years disdained advertising of any kind and fought to keep it far away. And many entrepreneurs who tried to sell something on the Net were thoroughly singed by angry flame-throwers. Some even had their E-mail capability dismantled as mailboxes were stuffed with angry missives. And we are talking tens of thousands of hot messages. But as the Internet has gone mainstream, most users are accepting the advertising and even shopping, especially women. Nothing should surprise you about that. Women have always had a sixth sense when it comes to finding a good deal. And what could be better than browsing (NOW we know why those Net searching tools are called "browsers") in the comfort of your own computer for anything you can think of, then buying it with the click of your helpful mouse. The Internet Shopping Network lists 600 companies. Check it out at http://www.internet.net.

We have mentioned the necessity for creativity in Internet advertising. Companies must provide interesting information as well as tout merchandise to keep people coming back to their home page advertisements. But this is a benefit from the consumer side of the monitor since it makes online shopping more fun. And shopping centers are springing up everywhere. Janice Castro writes in *Time* magazine about Cybermalls, a Vermont shopping center with nearly 60 online businesses. They keep their audience returning often because they offer free information on ski conditions and vacation resorts. Check this out at http://www.cybermalls.com/cymont/cymon-mal.htm (no "l" at the end!). Online shopping is just beginning, and interactive TV will no doubt up the stakes in the very near future.

Online shopping is similar to shopping from mail-order catalogs. And the mail-order business was a $57 billion industry in this country in 1995. Consumers are fond of purchasing things that don't need to be tried on or touched, like books, software, outdoor gear, and collectibles. Online shopping offers the important advantages of speed, convenience, selection, and price.

And if you're shopping for a vacation spot, you can't beat the advantages of being able to talk one-on-one with residents who live in the town you're thinking of visiting. "Where's the best spot for a quiet candlelit dinner and dancing?" you might ask. Even the chamber of commerce won't give you personal help like that. You can make plane, rental car, and hotel reservations online and get the lowest prices possible. And to get ready for your trip, you can order a new suitcase, a travel alarm clock, and some reading material all on your home computer. You can charge it on your credit card and have it shipped to your door right away.

Now, about using that credit card. You are no doubt wondering about the wisdom of sending your American Express numbers through the wild and woolly Internet channels. And businesses want to make this information secure, as well as authenticate your data and identity. These problems are being tackled by programmers working on encryption technology. Many businesses have such programs in place. Some consumers like to make prior arrangements by phone, regular mail, or fax with a vendor they want to use a lot—sort of a line of credit. And you can even use virtual money, or "E-cash," by opening an Internet bank account, then dragging and dropping a stack of coins into the vender's virtual hand. These transactions require special software, but it will no doubt be preloaded on the computers of the future. The ability to buy and sell easily on the Internet "is the key to unleashing the explosion in entrepreneurial commerce," says Magdelena Yesil, vice president for marketing of CyberCash, a company in the forefront of developing electronic cash.

Born2Shop: *Hello Virtual Vineyards? I'd like to order a case of Taittinger Champagne—at your special price, of course...:) Stand by for my check...I'm uploading it as we...uhh...speak...*

CutestClerk: *Yes, I see it! And we thank you for your business, Mrs. Born. Come back soon.*

Companies are streaming onto the Internet, and although many store fronts are still under construction, this is expected to be one of the world's largest and fastest growing markets. Following are some interesting places to shop on the Internet:

http://www.wwa.com/~bjcandy (Barbra Jean's Famous Candies)

http://www.usit.net/cafegour.html (Cafe Gourmet Coffees)

http://novaweb.com/lobster (Lobster Direct)

http://www.virtualvin.com (Virtual Vineyards)

http://www.digex.net/2xist,html (Men's Undies...:)

http://gate.cdworld.com/cdworld.html (Cdworld)

So, ladies, forget HarryHunk and let's go shopping!

8

Can We Play?

::: rolling the dice :::

Q. Dear Delilah,
Can I find some really wild and crazy games online?

Ray in NJ

A. Dear Ray,
Just how wild and crazy do you want to get?

Games are played online at all hours of the day and night. If you can't sleep, just boot up and jump into the night scene for some fun and games. Cyberspace is open round-the-clock, and there are ALL kinds of games, often very imaginative and so much fun that you will be wiping away the tears of laughter.

Who is playing? And what are they playing?

Everyone online seems to have a favorite pastime. Some just like to read outrageous newsgroup postings or watch others play. And some, probably the majority, enjoy actively participating in the craziness. The most popular BBSs or commercial services are those that let members engage in active chat with others. What they are playing is as varied as the people online. We'll begin with the more traditional games.

Dice

America Online, the "King o' Chat," has an automatic dice game that can be executed at any time by anyone in a lobby or room. It's called Six-Sided Dice and the "dice" can be rolled automatically by typing the command "//roll" and then hitting the return key. The screen will display the words "Screen name: rolled 2 six-sided dice 2 4" or something similar. The total of the dice is your score for that roll. The whole room can play, or just one person can roll to amuse himself or others in the room.

The most popular version of this game is strip dice and is played just like strip poker. This game is usually played in private rooms with just two participants. The object of the game is just what you think it is. The loser has to pull off an article of clothing and tell the other participant which item he or she has removed. The first person to be stripped of all clothing loses. From there the imagination takes over, and often, cybersex is the next step. (Is this what you mean, Ray?) When you are in a private room, anything goes. The system police, or Guides as they are called on this particular service, do not come into these rooms. They are, in fact, just that—*private* rooms.

Role Playing

This game involves people assuming the roles of others. You can be as creative as your mind will allow as you find yourself pretending to be a member of the opposite sex or in another age bracket or even living in another period of time.

There is a group who love to play in a medieval inn, where they can assume the roles of their favorite fantasy characters straight out of Robin Hood. They are kings or queens or noblemen, and they even bring magic into their stories. Story lines are intricate and inventive, and interesting people in real life are drawn into these games.

As you get to know one another online, real-life information is often exchanged and you may find yourself in the company of a judge, a pilot, a professor, or even a famous actress. Can you imagine being involved in a wonderful romantic fantasy, wooing a beautiful damsel with flowery words and using your magic sword to vanquish your rival? If you can, step on into the castle and meet the gang.

ChattyCathi once happened into a room called "Adult Babies." To her surprise, she found herself with a group pretending to be babies. One of the participants was describing himself as being dressed by his mother as a little girl in pinafore, lace-top socks, and T-strap flats any

little girl would adore. Good-natured kidding and creative dialogue completed the story, when one of the "babies" had to have his diaper changed. Hard to believe? Not to the millions playing online.

We will talk about gender bending—the ultimate in role playing—in a bit.

Weddings

Mock weddings take place online frequently. They are done in fun and are amusing to the participants as well as others in the room. An online wedding can be a logical extension of a romantic relationship that two people have, or it may not indicate any genuine interest outside the game. In fact, the participants have probably never met in real life but want to make a kind of commitment to a monogamous online relationship. Usually, there is much creative description and, of course, lots of tongue-in-cheek innuendo. These weddings have been presided over by real-life schoolteachers, attorneys, and bartenders. The descriptions of the setting, guests, and wedding attire can be hilarious. Delilah attended a wedding where the groom wore dress blues and tennis shoes and the bride wore nothing at all.

TerryTee tells of attending the online wedding of a man and woman in their real-life 50s. The bride and groom were online friends, and, in fact, the real-life husband of the bride was standing behind her telling her what to type onto her computer screen. You sure don't have to be young to have fun online.

Parties

The anonymity of online communication allows people to be as outrageous as they wish and yet permits them to

113

play safely. Genuine friendships have been made. There is
nothing quite like being a part of a group of people you
have never met in real life, from all over the country, happily engaged in a prank, birthday party, tavern free-for-all,
or wild scenario. The following spontaneous dialogue
happened when four online friends, BonnieBell, Jonny,
DaisyDee, and B-Man, invited a fifth friend, TonyT, to join
them in an imaginary double-wide trailer, up on blocks, in
a small Arkansas town. Tony, a definite Boston Yankee
and new to the online scene, was shocked at the wild dialogue that took place. Remember, these oniiners were really hundreds or thousands of miles apart, typing on their
individual computers. BonnieBell was typing from Austin,
B-man was in Little Rock, DaisyDee was in Cincinnati, and
Jonny was in Los Angeles. These players were in their 40s
and 50s, very literate, and clever. One even had a Ph.D.
(And, of course, Delilah did some editing.)

BonnieBell:	Thanks for letting my friend Tony, join us…
B-Man:	We are a friendly group. Hi Tony. C'mon in and take a load off.
DaisyDee:	I'll get more bean dip! :::::passing out iced tea in matching plastic cups from the Stop N Shop:::::::
Jonny:	Yep, we got lots of class, unless we're talking about sheep or goats…:) Hot damn…love a good goat!
B-Man:	All low-class…LOL
BonnieBell:	Well—you have to make do with what is available in ala. and ark.
B-Man:	Thas right.
TonyT:	Well, I don't know about sheep and goats. Don't you have women in ala. and ark.?
B-Man:	Sure, but WE like somethin' different now and agin.
Jonny:	Awww, quit braggin, B-Man.
DaisyDee:	B-Man graduated magna cum loaded from the U of A.

TonyT:	Maybe I'm at the wrong party.
B-Man:	And my best course was intercourse...all you hadda do was cum...:)
BonnieBell:	Don't be such a tight ass, Tony. These boys like their women a little on the trashy side. LOL
DaisyDee:	And B-Man likes his women in lotsa make-up...
TonyT:	I like sweet ladies...
BonnieBell:	With blue eyeliner?
B-Man:	Damn right. I got the hots for Tammy Faye fer sure.
BonnieBell:	And to think she was stuck with Jim.
DaisyDee:	I got really mad at B-Man—caught him putting my blue eyeliner on a chicken! I bit him on the arm.
Jonny:	Bet you'll hate to eat your favorite for dinner Thursday, B-Man.
TonyT:	Well, folks, thanks for showing me how Bama fans spend the weekend. Guess I'd better go look for a woman who likes the noncrude type. BYE
BonnieBell:	Bye Tony. Glad you came by for a lesson in southern hospitality.
Jonny:	Now that he's gone, let's all get NEKID...
DaisyDee:	We already are—nekid as jaybirds...
B-Man:	And if the kids come in, we can tell 'em we gave our clothes to the Good Will.
BonnieBell:	You know, Tony won't forget this evening soon.
B-Man:	Probably not in this lifetime!
Jonny:	It is hard to be in middle-aged puberty and have teenagers...they don't buy the lies...:)

And so on and so on...

Mind Games

Onliners are having lots of fun. They are playing mind games. And if you run into the lothario or the gender bender, as we describe them next, don't be disappointed when the truth comes out. Delilah has created this guide to show the positive and fun side of connecting online, and there is no safer place to experiment with anything that suits your fancy. Just remember to tell your friends who and what you really are before you plan a real-life get-together! You may not want someone to really fall in love with you or to hurt your new friend, who is expecting Dan when Danielle shows up.

The Lothario or Lotharianna   *Webster's Dictionary* defines "lothario" as "a lighthearted seducer of women." And there are a lot of men and women online who like to try out their charms and sexy words on the many eager partners they find in cyberspace. Onliners just out for a good time may have no desire for anything more than the chase and conquest. An example is the man who made arrangements to meet three different women in one city on the same weekend. All three thought he cared deeply for them. They had spent considerable time chatting with him online and even talked with him on the telephone. He didn't show up on the appointed weekend, but three angry women DID meet each other and decided to have coffee together to plan their revenge!

Babs had a way with words and had numerous online boyfriends. But her reputation soon preceded her, and the game lost its charm, for her *and* her friends. Some women like to lead men on just for fun. Don't let it get out of hand. Fess up before you hurt someone.

The Gender Bender   Haven't you always wondered what it would be like to be the opposite sex? Well, here's your chance. It's fun to assume the opposite role once in awhile, and it can be the height of creativity. You can pretend to wear a dress or experiment with undergarments you have only imagined. Or you might enjoy being "one of the boys" and talking about sports, beer, or women. Most who do this are quite harmless. But if you are interested in meeting someone with whom you might form a lasting relationship, this is probably not the best way.

Beth made arrangements to meet Raye, her online one and only, to find that this wonderful man, to whom she had spent hours typing sexy chat, was really a woman. They later admitted that they felt so drawn to each other, in a deeply mental way, that their actual gender didn't matter. Hmmmmmm...again, something for everyone.

Gender bending became a topic of conversation in a room one night, and a woman in the room laughed and said that the simplest way to find out if you are talking with a woman is to ask what size panties, or "seat covers," she wears. When asked why, she promptly replied that most men don't have a clue how women's underwear is sized and would probably answer that she wore a size 24, or something similar, when, in fact, the correct answer would be size 5 or 6. And within a week, one of the people who had been in the room remarked that this very situation had arisen and when he asked the question, the answer was a dead giveaway. LOL

Domination/submission: Sadomasochism

Some of the cleverest and often the most risqué scenarios are played out in the dungeons, chateaus, and castles online, which are known for these alternative life-style fun and games. (Perhaps THIS is what you are looking for, Ray.) If you want to learn about the best leather restraints, body piercing, slave management, or various types of whips, this could be just the ticket. "These games let you fantasize about something you might not want to do in real life," stated CherryPit. "Online, you can safely explore another side to your sexual nature," agreed DomTom. There are BBSs that specialize in various forms of these activities, often taking it offline into real-life parties and get-togethers.

The English Palace, a BBS in Hazlet, New Jersey, will sell you a 6-month membership for $50.00, and Master Charles maintains the largest fetish library in the country. He cracks his whip to keep the wilder de Sades in line, and lots of women play here too.

If you are using Microsoft Windows extensions and have a soundcard (Soundblaster seems to be the industry favorite) and speakers, you can add hearable sound files to your playtime. On AOL, sound files are those that end with the filename extension .WAV and are called *waves*. Adding the wave file {S whip to your personal wave collection will allow you to hear the sound of a whip cracking. Everyone online with you who has the same file will also hear the whip crack as your typed {S whip appears on their screens. You can even make sound files in your own voice, using a microphone. These are happily shared, traded, and collected. Wouldn't it be fun to send a sound file to your online master in your own voice saying, "I submit to you. Do with me what you wish?" :) More about sound files later.

Before choosing a specialized BBS, you might want to play in the larger online services to see what suits your fancy. On the large services most of the really interesting action takes place in private rooms, and there are special rooms that meet at prescribed times, where a password or individual invitation may be necessary to enter. The following dialogue will give you some idea of what to expect.

MastrMATE: Hello my little pet...how are you today?

subliMATE: :::kneeling before my Master::::: I am well, sir, and you are also, I trust?

MastrMATE: I am more than a little displeased with you, I'm afraid. You failed to perform your exercises properly this morning, didn't you? Tell the truth, now...

subliMATE: :::::::bowing head in shame::::: Yes, Master, but however did you know?

MastrMATE:	*You know better than to try to deceive me. Now you must be punished. Remove all your clothes—*QUICKLY.
subliMATE:	But Master…
MastrMATE:	{S whip *You must learn to be obedient. We have been over all this before. :::::approaching my sub with whip snapping:::::*
subliMATE:	*:::::quickly undressing::::::: I am doing as you request, Sir. You are my Master and I want to please you in all things…*
MastrMATE:	GET DOWN ON ALL FOURS
subliMATE:	*Yessir… ::::quickly dropping to the floor:::::*
MastrMATE:	*:::::::CRACK, SNAP:::::::::I am only going to give you two smart licks. This will show you that I do appreciate your quick obedience.*
subliMATE:	Thank you, Sir.

And so on and so on…:)

Often a master, or Dom, will have a carefully negotiated contract with his sub, in writing, to make the roles clear. And, although many keep these games only online, for some the point will be to meet in real life to continue the game, even making it a real life-style. And the master can be male OR female (Domme). In fact, the true Dommes are in the most demand as there seem to be many more men and women who like to be subs. "Lots of people with high-powered careers during the day enjoy letting someone else make all their decisions—take charge of them—in their playtime," said Fuzzysub.

A typical contract between a Dom and sub might look something like this:

TERMS and CONDITIONS of Your Obedience

PREAMBLE

I understand there is a difference between pain and torture. I will never inflict pain or humiliate capriciously.

My subs are witty and intelligent and understand that some pain and humiliation must necessarily be a part of effective training.

Since my subs are witty and intelligent, independent thoughts may be expressed; hence, there is always the need for retraining to refresh the understanding of the need for obedience.

I will gladly answer any questions about the theory of obedience but never any about my actions. Those are FORBIDDEN.

TERMS

You will obey all instructions without objection, delay, or excuse.

You will not anticipate my wishes. You will do only as you are told when you are told.

You will not jump to any conclusions about my acts or activities.

You will at all times show me the common courtesies expected, including making all arrangements for planned activities and dealing with all petty details of those activities.

You will never display anger or frustration. The only emotions you may display are obeisance and pleasure.

Unless out in the general public, you will never use my name; you will address me as "Sir" at all times.

When and if the time comes that you've earned the right to call me Master, you will then do so.

Other than when you are having your period, you may not wear underwear at any time.

You will keep your legs spread at all times when talking to me on the phone, when we are seated alone, and when you are online under your sub name.

You will masturbate as required, at least daily, and keep a log, detailing times of day, methods, all fantasies, length and intensity of orgasm. In your logs, you will explain details explicitly and completely.

Anytime we are together, in person or on the phone or online, you will ask permission to come.

While no other submissive will have precedence over you as long as our relationship continues, I will terminate the relationship rather than diminish your status. I may at anytime accept another female's submission for training or other reasons. You will accept this and give me guidance.

Whenever we are alone together, the first thing you will do is kneel before me, head bowed, and state the following: "Sir, I submit to you, I am here only to serve you. My only desire is to obey you and please you. I accept your domination. Do with me as you please." Upon my acceptance of your obeisance, you will immediately undress and stand before me, head bowed, awaiting my wishes, unless I tell you otherwise.

No excuses will be accepted and disobedience will be cause for punishment and/or dismissal.

xxx

Whewwwww. Well, whatever floats your boat. (And now you know, Ray.)

How can I find the sexy pictures (GIFs, JPGs, etc.)?

To enhance your online experience with all the photographic files available on the Internet, you might like to add graphic capability to your system. (State-of-the-art computer systems have everything built right in!) It is by no means essential but adds a new level to the fun and games. GIF stands for Graphics Interchange Format, a CompuServe developed and copyrighted format for viewing graphics, first released in 1987. It is pronounced "jif" by most people. Although there are other graphic formats, such as TIF and JPG, GIF files are popular because they can be used with several types of computer: PC, Macintosh, Amiga, and AppleII. This format also accommodates monochrome or color graphics of any size and complexity.

GIF files are self-compressed, and it takes only a few minutes to download one. A GIF is like a slide, but instead of a slide projector to view it, it needs a GIF projector, called a viewer. There are many viewer programs available. Two popular ones are Paint Shop Pro and CompuShow. Your online services know you will want to see pictures, so they have provided shareware programs, which you may download into your system free or for a nominal fee. Some services have this downloading procedure so smoothly interfaced that you just click your mouse on the "download" box and the picture appears.

To make this simple, let's suppose you want to send a picture of yourself to your favorite online buddy. You must put that wonderful photograph on a disk so that you can upload it into your system. A floppy disk can hold five or ten pictures, but the more on a disk, the lower their quality. If you are verrrry well set up and knowledgeable, you can scan your picture onto a disk yourself, using a device called a scanner. More about scanners in a moment. If you don't have your own scanner, you may take your photo to your local full-service computer store or photo center that has a scanning service and ask them to make a GIF for you. Delilah took a photograph of the students in the computer communication class she teaches and an empty disk to the local Kinko shop, sat down with Lauri, and asked to have the picture made into an IBM-compatible file in GIF format. It was done in a matter of minutes, for a nominal fee.

After you have your disked photo, you copy it into your system and are ready to send it on to whomever you wish. Delilah uploaded it through her online service to each of her students to surprise them. What fun it is to watch photographs appear for the first time! Many BBSs have picture galleries of members who have uploaded their photographs.

If you find that you enjoy photographs and want to make your own GIFs, you can get your own scanner. A quality scanner looks like a small copying machine. There are also hand-held scanners available that resemble the mouse on your computer. If you have an image-processing program, you can manipulate or enhance your photograph before sending it to your friend or bulletin board gallery. Some scanners capture only black and white images, but the more expensive ones can also capture color.

Never send any pictures that you don't own the legal rights to

Newspapers are filled with stories of people getting caught for illegally copying, sending, or selling graphics to others. When a member of a major online service uploads a picture, he or she is taking full legal responsibility for any copyright infringement situation which may arise. America Online says, "The uploader is entirely responsible for any repercussions, financial, legal or otherwise, stemming from files they supply to the America Online services."

This brings us to the area of pornography. Unfortunately, there are those members of family-oriented online services who want to use them for sending pornographic pictures. This is strongly discouraged by these major services, as we have said, though there are certainly BBSs that do specialize in this type of activity. The problem is that it is hard to police pornography online and stop anyone who may be so inclined. In time, there will, no doubt, be cybercops tracking down these rule breakers and issuing them citations and warnings, perhaps even giving them tickets! Although this subject is hotly discussed in the media, only about 1 percent of the material available on the Internet has anything of a pornographic nature (as Andrew Kantor states in the October 1995 issue of *Internet World* magazine), and this material is much more difficult to access than your local magazine rack. But families that share computer time should discuss this—set some guidelines and limits. If your interest is in pornography, Delilah suggests you use the proper service or BBS for this. They are listed in many computer books and magazines.

Commercial services may have guidelines similar to the following: "Do not upload so-called adult, R-rated or X-rated files. In simplest terms, 'absolutely no frontal nudity, genitalia, sex acts, or morally objectionable material.' " However, as we have mentioned, this is hard to police and these files do abound on many online services.

America Online also has a "Parental Control" feature that can be accessed easily when you click on the word "Member" at the main screen. This enables the master account holder to restrict access to certain areas and features, like chat and Internet newsgroups. It can be set for one or all screen names on the account. Once this parental control feature has been set for a particular screen name, it is active each time that screen name signs on. This enables parents to block activities or areas they feel might be inappropriate for their children.

Since the dawn of humanity, sex has had an unusually active creative impact on the development of technology. When the telescope was invented, what did humans want to look at? Their neighbors undressing! Sex has always been one of the first uses for any new invention. Nicholson Baker, author of *Vox,* a novel about telephone sex, says, "We're always looking for exotic new ways of doing the same old things. New technologies are strange and exciting, and one wants romance to be strange and exciting." And Walter Kendrick, author of *The Secret Museum: Pornography in Modern Culture,* says "Pornography is always unsatisfied. It's always a substitute for the contact between two bodies." And since men, traditionally the ones most interested in pornography, are the chief enthusiasts for new gadgets, it follows that they would quickly adapt their computers to the enjoyment of pornographic GIFs. Although there seem to be lots more men online sending GIFs and interested in hot chat, PuppyDawg, an online friend, told Delilah that he couldn't believe how many women were asking him to participate in phone sex after chatting online. The women online who are enjoying GIFs tailor-made for them say, "Thank you, MUSCLES! We've come a long way, Baby!"

(Check out Appendix B for Delilah's favorite bulletin board services.)

*Where can I find the sounds (*WAVs*)?*

Now let's look at sounds online. New PCs and Macintosh computers have built-in speakers and sound drivers as part of their multimedia packages. You can always open your machine's case and see if you have a speaker, but generally you will know right away because your computer will "talk" to you. To get state-of-the-art sounds that are compatible with your online service, you may need to purchase extra hardware—a soundboard (also called a soundcard) and more speakers. There are several good soundboard makers—SoundBlaster, Media Vision, and UltraSound are a few—but you should choose a board that is SoundBlaster-compatible since that is the current standard everyone uses. Once you slip your soundboard into the proper port, you open up the possibility of all sorts of sounds.

The major sound formats are .VOCC, .SOU, .SND, and .WAV. And since most Windows applications require .WAV files (called waves), you may need special software to convert your sound files. Online you can send and receive sound files while chatting with your friends. But your online friend must have the same sound file in his or her system to hear the identical sound that you do, and these files are uploaded and downloaded just like other files. Online services have libraries full of music and comments (like "ouch") that you can download. Or, with a microphone, you can custom-make your own sounds and upload them to your friends. You can then type {S cmere, and everyone online with whom you've shared your file will hear your voice say, "Come on over here, darlin'," or whatever you have recorded. Some onliners specialize in making and sharing wave files, and there are hundreds of common ones circulating. Of course, there are a number of risqué sounds circulating. {S rollhay is a nasal female voice saying, "Hello. Would you like to have a roll in the hay?" When you see the bracket and *S* before a word, you will know it is a wave file being played. If it looks interesting to you, you might say, "What is that sound? Can you send it to me? I will send you something in return."

Before long, you will have more sound files than you can remember. Often, they are snippets of favorite songs or parts from movies, and they usually take a minute or two to upload (send) or download (receive). Many onliners like to have a special signature sound they play when they log onto their online service, and the Over Forty gang on America Online play {PR ("So this is where you guys went") when they enter a private room they use, called "OFUG" at the time of this writing. It's a sort of password. (They are a friendly bunch and won't mind if you stop in…:)

If this sounds like fun to you, you should enjoy this little story, using lots of sound files. Many of your online friends will have these and will be happy to share. Or stop by Delilah's World Wide Web site to pick 'em up. The address is http://www.delilah.com/askme.

WAVs World

{S higuys
{S ltsparty

Lulu smiled broadly at the group, as she moved quickly toward the last chair in the room. Suddenly her path was blocked by the biggest man she had ever seen. He moved his arm and…

{S whipcrack

{S hurt...she said.
{S nextluv...he said.

As he reached for her, she smoothly sidestepped and placed her hands on her hips.

{S watch

Lulu knew that the whole room was watching and enjoying this little scenario. Just more online fun and games.

"I could let my big dog loose on you, yaknow, Bucko," she said feigning bravado.

{S woof

He looked at her soooooo smirkingly...

{S YRS
{S nevermind...she said.
{S getalife

With that she flounced to her seat, then noticed the tall, handsome man in the shadows.

{S cowboy
{S big-gun
{S chuckle

Nowwww THIS was more like it! A man with some style!

{S lap

"Let's have a drink, Babygirl," he drawled.

{S drink

He took her hand and led her up the stairs to the loft.

{S again
{S precious

Soon they were rolling together on the huge round bed that filled the softly lighted loft.

{S naked

What a find he was!
What a find she was!

{S organism (Nope, this isn't misspelled!)

Suddenly, she jumped up and pulled on her cyberboots.

{S time

My five kids and husband will soon be home wanting their real-time suppers! I have to microwave some hot dogs. Thanks for a great time-out!

{S bye
{S kiss

THE GAMEBOX

WAVcollection—Collect 20 favorite wave files for your own collection. Send 'em and share 'em.

Where is the gay community playing?

Fortunately, life online is just as varied and colorful as real life. Not all people want the same things, and there are forums for gays, lesbians, and bisexuals online as well as meeting places for transvestites or transsexuals. Discussing sex on a computer with someone can have an uplifting effect and can even be educational and healthy. All the photographs, stories, and paraphernalia you could ever want can be found online. Bulletin board services where gays and lesbians who might feel isolated in their communities can find a welcoming place to meet others are very popular, and we will look at a couple.

There are thousands of adult BBSs in the United States alone, but The Backroom, in Brooklyn, New York, insists it is the premier gay BB on the East Coast. You can find the latest information on gay and health-related news items here, as well as conference areas for lesbians and gay men involved in relationships with straight men and women.

On the West Coast, check out Eye Contact, San Francisco's largest gay men's online service. You can even search for the lover of your dreams here, as well as join in discussions about everything and anything. Sysop Richard Kravitz says, "We offer a safe haven for gay men, a place to play and meet like-minded people."

To gain access to some adult BBSs, you must be 21 years of age or older and provide proof of age. And hot chat seems to be a staple of most. You need never be at a loss for someone to talk to again. And you may just find that special, deep relationship everyone hopes for.

On one of the large online services, special rooms are set up for individuals enjoying alternative life-styles. They are labeled as such and are listed on the roster so that you know what you are getting into when you enter. Some have names like "New York f for f" or "Gay Guys Get Together." It is assumed that you want this kind of chat and action when you "walk through the door."

If someone you meet seems interesting, you might approach him or her with a private message to ask if there is any interest in a personal conversation. On the large services, those teens who might be exploring their sexuality can find a place to talk and play. It is a good, safe place to check out the bisexual scene, and there are many support groups available. Perhaps having an online group of friends can be a first step out of the closet.

Where is the REALLY weird stuff?

What is weird for one person might not be weird for another, but surely we have covered your question, Ray!

Let's click into the Internet one more time. Many insist that the ultimate in sexual diversion can be found on the IRC, the Internet Relay Conference, the world's largest system, with chatters from all over the world. There can be 3,000 participants at any one time, in all time zones, from 150 countries, chatting all day and all night. Lots of conversations about things "weird" here.

Hundreds of new Internet web sites are popping up every day. And sometimes they disappear just as fast. The Pleasure Palace will give you phone sex in many languages. Their address is:

http://www.hk.super.net/~palace/.

And for an online beauty pageant go to:

http://www.tyrell.net/~robtoups/BABE.html.

Whewww!

Nonsexual but weird pages abound too. If you check out http://www.ama.caltech.edu/~mrm/godzilla.html, you can find out everything you ever wanted to know about Godzilla. And if you want a weird love letter to send, check out http:www.nando.net/toys/cyrano.html. At this page you answer a few questions and they then compose something for you...:) Or you can skip all these pages and go right to Mirsky's Worst of the Web at http://turn-pike.net/metro/mirsky/Worst.html.

Internet newsgroups also provide interesting reading and postings. The following is from Tammy:

> **Subject:** TAMMY WANTS TO BE SPANKED
>
> *I'm 23 years old, 5'8", weigh 125, and I have been a bad girl. I think I could benefit from a good spanking. Are you interested? Tammy*

Tammy got lots of replies. This one is from Myke:

> *Tammy—I am a 39-year-old, black, ex-marine in OK. I will spank your naughty bare bottom over my knee when you tell me just how bad you have been. Let me know when and where.*

We will end this walk on the weird side with a look at fetishes. Delilah's old and well-used dictionary defines "fetish" as "an object held sacred—often unreasonably so—by savage or barbarous peoples." Is this a new label for onliners?

On just one day the following fetishes were discussed in the alt.sex.fetish newsgroup:

ballet-style boots

sex potions

ladies clothing (wet and dry)—made out of nylon, leather, fur, silk, plastic, and rubber

German WWII uniforms

body painting

heavy exotic makeup

90210

business suits and ties

And everyone knows there are lots of REALLY kinky fetishes in the world, especially in the world of cyberspace. There are even bulletin board services that specialize...:) Here are some of the fetishes the "barbarous" people online enjoy:

big-busted, lactating women

body piercing and manipulation

bondage and bondage devices, such as hand and ankle cuffs, black leather costumes, and stiletto high heels

spanking

enemas

semi-public sex

flashing

If one of these is just the ticket for you, check out the following BBSs:

1. **Aline, NewCom LINK BBS**—a product of France's Minitel Services Company and represented in the United States by the New York-based Newcom Link Co. This BBS is an adult board with a definite international flavor. On Aline, you can find people anxious

to talk to you about restaurants and movies, as well as fetishes and sex games. You can also practice your French, as the French practice on you! Phone No. 1-800-272-8737.

2. **Star BBS Network**—located in New Jersey, offers a place where singles and couples can play in special areas for cross-dressers and S&M afficionados. This BBS offers chat, games, and conferences with others around the world. Phone No. 1-800-521-2733.

3. **Odyssey**—This Los Angeles BBS offers live chat, a large GIF library, games, travel services, a matchmaking service, and forums for D/s activities. It is a popular meeting place for those into alternative lifestyles. Phone No. 1-800-947-0936.

Appendix C gives you Delilah's Internet Newsgroup picks and check out Appendix D for her favorite World Wide Web sites.

9

Looking for Love?

:::uploading Delilah's 10 steps:::

Q. Dear Delilah,
Is online love only screen deep?

AnxiousAngel

A. Dear Angel,
I think it's what you make it. The words of Somerset Maugham
seem particularly apt: "Love is what happens to a man and
woman who don't know each other." :)

For some people, playing on their computers is just a time-out. But for others it can be deeply meaningful, a new road to understanding another person, a first step on the path to a love relationship. The secret to finding real love lies in each individual. SwgBirches, an online friend to many, says, "Buried deep within the play and format, centered and weighted, balanced and unbent, must be the truth. Words must be made to count." Remember, when you really care about someone online, you keep your promises and commitments.

Can I really find love in cyberspace?

Yes you can. Many people of all ages have told Delilah their stories. And since colleges and universities all over the world are connected to the Internet, students seem particularly open to the possibility of meeting someone special on their computers. At the University of Kentucky, KD met Becky, also a UK student. They enjoyed chatting so much, they decided to meet for coffee the next day, and KD proposed to Becky only five days later. "She just said the right things to me. It can be difficult at a large university to find others that you have a lot in common with, especially if you are older than most of the other students. I met six or seven girls before Becky, and she probably met ten guys. But we knew right away that we would like each other. It's a great way to get to know someone before you meet them f2f. We met, fell in love and are very happy."

It works for many people outside school settings too.

Love on the I-way

Waffles, a Chicago stock broker, met his online sweetie in Dallas after months of E-mail messages. He even moved his business to Dallas, and they recently married. "We felt as though we really knew each other well when we met in person, and trust had been established."

A typical scenario might unfold in this manner: Anne, using her pseudonym AnnieFannie, boots up her computer in her office every afternoon after work to relax for a few minutes and chat with fellow onliners she finds in the "Pub." Today, she finds herself chatting with a man named TrueNBlue. They exchange pleasantries, a few witty comebacks, and find they are enjoying each other. They then ask for more personal information, like age, where each lives, and perhaps even physical descriptions. When it is time to sign off, they promise to look for each other again. After several similar sessions, if they feel drawn to each other—if they have "clicked" with each other—TrueNBlue might ask Annie for her phone number so they can chat one to one. This is a big step for Annie. But her apprehensions are overcome by the bond of friendship forming, and they chat on the telephone for two hours the first night. The next day they find they can't wait until they can boot up and get down to a meaningful exchange. After several days or weeks of conversation, they know much about each other, including real names and addresses. Perhaps photos or tapes of favorite music have rounded out the mental picture. If feelings are intense and curiosity is highly aroused, they will probably decide to meet. Usually the man will go to the woman, and if the emotion is still strong, they could find they are talking about love to each other.

After this exciting first real-life meeting, a period of time to really get to know each other is recommended. This might last for months or even years. But if they have found true, real-life love, they will end up walking down that rose-strewn aisle together. And what makes this blossoming love story really unique is that Annie can live in Washington State and her new friend can live across the continent in New York State. They would never have met each other if not for this new technology linking them at their desks every day.

What about love in a friendship?

Delilah believes there are many kinds of love, and a really special love can happen between people online, a kind of deep friendship, only more profound. Perhaps we are at the cutting edge of something new, a kind of relationship we will need a new word for—being "lined," instead of being "loved." It's a wonderful kind of love that bypasses the superficial, and who's to say that it's any less real when transmitted over telephone lines and downloaded into our magical computers than if it were to develop from a face-to-face encounter.

Many onliners have experienced this special friendship and go out of their way to express it. Marcia was surprised and delighted to receive lovely roses from Karen after sharing her postsurgery blues online. And Kevin was deeply moved when Todd helped him write a resume for a new job. Sandra and John had an online wedding, a union not uncommon, as we have mentioned, when two people enjoy sharing their lives online and want to commit to a sort of monogamous relationship. An online marriage can be a kind of test-drive for some.

It doesn't seem to matter that these people have not met each other in real life and perhaps never will. They have found special rewards in their online relationships—unparalleled honesty, refreshing creativity, and unencumbered good humor. The feelings are real and touching in a very deep way.

Stories of these loving friendships, or cybertales, abound online. And the roads on which these stories move are the many computer bulletin board systems all over the world. As we have said, millions of people are talking online. And they are telling their true stories, stories that can bring sympathy, criticism, or laughter. The WELL, that popular bulletin board based north of San Francisco, is considered by many to be the creative and spiritual home of the computer culture. Here people discuss parenting, poetry, AIDS, sex, religion, aging, and anything else having to do with real life experiences. The stories are simple and often very touching. Everyone here feels they have a concerned audience, and people exposed to these stories do care and do respond. And the WELL is just one forum.

Even in the large commercial online services there are genuine loving friendships. A caring and concerned woman in Florida writes daily letters of sympathy, praise, or concern to a large group of fellow onliners. She expresses a real concern for her fellows. "Let's all keep RIPTIDE in our prayers. He just found out he has multiple myeloma, a type of bone cancer, and would love encouraging E-mail from all of you." Many messages came pouring to RIPTIDE. He had more friends than he knew.

Another story from CompuServe began, "Do you have any idea what it is like to be gay?" This onliner tells of being mercilessly beat up by a group of soldiers. And a sympathetic reply from a concerned soldier began, "I was very touched by your message, buddy. That's not what I lost three toes for in Vietnam. I fought so you could do whatever you wanted so long as you didn't hurt anybody."

We have only just begun to explore the possibilities of sharing and caring via computers. The ill connect with one another; employers find employees; people find friends; and some find connections that develop into real-life, more traditional and romantic, love relationships.

Why does this work?

It's not all an accident. If you are looking for a love relationship, it needs to be nurtured online, just as in real life. So let's start at the beginning—that first online date. It can be the beginning of something very wonderful.

Dating on your computer is not unlike real-life dating. A marvelous date should be planned or thought out carefully. Psychiatrists and psychologists tell us that passion can result from play. And a date that is carefully planned to include play and fun can lead to something serious and meaningful. So when you plan what your date on the computer will entail, try to heighten sensations and the feeling of romance. Part of the fun is in the planning.

Begin with good conversation—the heart of a good date. Think about an interesting topic of conversation before you boot up for a conversation online. Look through a current newspaper—all it takes is a fresh idea or a funny story—and you are on your way. Good conversation in a room full of people can lead to a "Yes" answer when you ask someone special to step into a private room to talk alone. Ferinstance...

James:	I just read in the newspaper that by the year 1999 there will 22.5 million households subscribing to an online service or an Internet provider. That's lots more than today's 8.5 million!
Jan:	WOW—so many people to talk to and so little time!
James:	Well, actually, it's always more fun to talk to just one person...
Jan:	You are right about that...the fun for me is getting to know someone well...:)
James:	Would you like to step into my private "office" so we can explore this thought?
Jan:	ok

Once more, Delilah reminds you to always be truthful online. If you need to embellish a funny story to get the point across, that's one thing. But if you are seriously involved with someone in real life, or even married, you should make this clear in the beginning. If you mislead your "date" about your age or appearance, this will come back to haunt you later also. Your path to a deeper relationship can be shut down very quickly if you are deceptive. Remember, playing games online is a good way to discern truths.

THE GAMEBOX

Truth—This popular online game works like this: One person asks the other if he or she wants to play a game, to set the stage. Then the ground rules are explained. Each person can ask the other one question, but the answer must be truthful. If the truth is too difficult at this stage, one can take a pass and accept another question. Simple questions, like favorite foods or music, can lead to more interesting questions about hopes and feelings. After hours of conversation, a good question might be "Tell me something you have never told anybody before." A game of **Truth** can last for weeks...:)

Just as in real life, a good relationship is built on words: you have to *say* how you feel. And showing appreciation for your online partner's sensitivity or cleverness is essential. Deeper feelings are born in the appreciation two people have for each other. After you have described what you are wearing, hearing the words "You have a wonderful sense of style" makes you feel truly special, even if you are in that old blue bathrobe...:) (As technology advances and we can actually see each other on our computers, we will have to dress up to boot up!)

Tom T., an ol' country boy, likes to use the element of

surprise in his online conversations. Just as in real life, a surprise can have an extraordinary effect. Using computer symbols to make pictures can supply this added dimension. Eyes (o)(o) can be carefully watching an online partner. If you have the software allowing you to draw a picture on your computer, you can use the file-sending capability of your BBS to send a carefully drawn bouquet of flowers to your new online sweetie. Or go into Flowernet, a WWW shopping mall based in the UK, and send a dozen real roses to surprise that special someone (http://mkn.co.uk).

Real-life marriage proposals have even been made, and accepted, online. The following were taken from an active bulletin board:

Subject: Suggestions Please!
From: Steverino

Please help. I have proposed informally online. She accepted! Now I need a very special and romantic way to formally propose in person.

Subj: Suggestions
From: SpicyLady

Congratulations on your engagement! How about taking her out to dinner and giving her a rose with an engagement ring attached? Or, better yet, give her the ring sweetly nestled inside a box of computer disks!

And to keep your feet on the ground, here is another posting:

Subj: Nightmares/Dreams
From: LatinLovr

I recently met someone from online and it was a complete nightmare! No chemistry, no attraction (even though we had exchanged pictures)...a complete waste of time. BUT I am going to meet someone else in a few weeks from online and am very optimistic about it. You can't let one bad experience keep you from making new friends. Maybe I am a helpless romantic...who knows? :)

In an online discussion, one lovely spring morning with love in the air, a popular woman online compared her interpretation of online mindmates with the ancient theory of twin souls. This gives us a good understanding of what happens when two people fall in love on their computers. "Twin Souls rush together in recognition, ignoring all convention and custom, all social rules of behavior, driven by an inner knowing too overwhelming to be denied. No one can break the tie between Twin Souls, not even themselves. The bond may be weakened, the final union and consummation delayed, but they cannot be separated permanently." During the careful search for one's mindmate, there are many side trips (relationships that appear to be genuine), but they may fade into disinterest or boredom. Often there are complications, or even pain, but finally when the lonely and separated mindmates are united, the pieces of life's jigsaw puzzle form into a complete picture. Don't you think the ancient Greek writer Aristophanes would have loved computers?

A word to the wise: Keep in mind that it is very easy to misjudge another person online. As we said earlier, some essential elements of face-to-face communication are missing: gestures, body language, and posture. The advantages of online communication—immediacy, intimacy, and anonymity—can become disadvantages very quickly. Remember, you can't take back what you have said. And you certainly don't want to get into a flame war. You will never take that first step to romance if you are not polite and considerate.

Above all, listen carefully. Bernie Zilbergeld, author of *The New Male Sexuality,* says, "Your one and only job, while listening, is to understand the other's experience, feelings, attitude, or point of view." While listening, you should be quiet until you really understand what the other is saying. This is especially true in computer communication, where instead of listening you are reading.

Don't hurry an online conversation. Give your online

partner time to respond to you. Sometimes you may sit and wait for several seconds. When Karen P. on CompuServe is angry at something Roger has said, she types verrrry slowly. And if you must leave the keyboard for a few minutes, be sure to tell your partner you will BRB. As in real-time conversation, when in doubt, ask a question. Roger usually says "HUH?"

It is wonderful to be able to express your thoughts openly within the intimate and anonymous framework that online communication offers. Surprise your online friend with a macro, or automatic text (a phrase repeated over and over with a single keystroke). Software programs like Powertools allow you to make your own macros, so Jj can type "My love has entered the room" over and over instantly when he notices TexasLov enter the room on America Online.

Jj: *My love has entered the room.*
        My love has entered the room.
        My love has entered the room.
        My love has entered the room.

TomTom on Prodigy says, "All relationships take time. And patience is indeed a virtue in cyberspace."

What are Delilah's 10 steps to online love?

If you hope to find a love online that might develop into a real-life relationship, consider the following 10 steps. They have worked for lots of people online.

1. Be open to the possibility (or possibilities).

2. Plan consistent online time. (Think of this as an investment.)

3. Ask questions. (And hear what isn't said.)

4. Be truthful. (BE TRUTHFUL—for the umpteenth time!)

5. Be playful and witty and let your intelligence show. (This isn't really so difficult.)

6. Don't chase too hard; be a bit mysterious. (But DO chase.)

7. Get to know someone well before giving out personal information. (We've plowed this ground enough!)

8. Talk on the telephone and send pictures (or music, flowers, candy, mementos, etc.).

9. Meet in a public place (not the No-Tell Motel!).

10. Start all over in the real world (or log back onto your computer to try again!).

Now, suppose you have completed these steps. You have fallen in love with your computer friend, a love that makes your heart sing. You feel happy, young, and sexy. Is it real? You want to put it into words:

10 Reasons Why I Love You

1. Your open sincerity/honesty

2. Your quick wit

3. Your sense of humor

4. Your sweetness

5. Your kindness

6. Your genuine concern for me

7. Your ability to express your emotions

8. Your sexy thoughts

9. All the things we have in common

10. And something totally irrational and completely unexplainable

In the end, you really can't explain love. You have to experience it. If this expresses your feelings, you are in love. Have fun with all this. That's part of the magic. It should be great fun.

Douglas Coupland, in his book *microserfs*, writes of a couple who find love online. In this book, Amy insists that "interfacing with Michael over the Net was the only way she could ever really know that he was talking to 'her,' not with his concept of her."

Can we come to the wedding?

There are two kinds of weddings that can result from a computer relationship:

1. "virtual," or pretend

2. real-life, or traditional

Virtual weddings, as described earlier, can be a fun game for both the happy couple and the guests.

THE GAMEBOX

The Wedding Game—Have a pretend wedding in front of a special group of online friends in an imaginary setting late at night or early in the morning, when the invited guests can be present. Make it elaborate, with special invitations, flowers, and gifts of poems or special stories. How about a sunrise wedding on a California beach, including music WAV files that can be circulated among the guests? Careful descriptions of attire

> and food can enhance this scenario.
>
> BTW—these marriages are easily undone if the partners have a fight. One of the partners simply says "I divorce thee" three times! And you pay only for the fun part, in connect charges to your online service or BBS.

People who have found special relationships on their computers insist that the electronic world is a perfect place for romance because electronic communities are a fantasy world and fantasy is at the heart of any great romance. JasonK met Sandy late one night when he couldn't sleep. He described taking her out for an early breakfast at the local all-night cafe in his small California town. He ordered for her and described the steaming coffee and a beautiful omelet. They laughed together and discovered they had much in common. They have been meeting to chat on their computers several times a week since that early breakfast and have recently decided to talk on the phone. Jason would like to meet Sandy and hopes to get together with her on his upcoming trip to Chicago. Will their friendship turn into a real romance? Only time will tell. It is certainly a possibility, one that didn't exist a few short years ago.

If you want your online relationship to lead to a real-life wedding—a mortgage, children, and joint bank accounts— you might decide to use Lucy and Robert as models. Robert proposed to Lucy online, and this is their story:

Lucy Donovan lives in Nashville. She met Robert T. in March. Since he lives in New Jersey, they would never have met had they not been living in the computer age. In August he popped the question online in a lovely E-mail letter.

> *You have become the light in my life. I look for you every day and need your messages more than you realize. I am a new man since we met online, and when I got your first photograph, I knew you were the one for me. I got to know you from the inside out—*

fell in love with your happy personality and funny sense of humor. We have shared our deepest thoughts, have spent hours talking to each other about everything and anything. You know my moods, can sense when I need a hug or kind word. In so many ways we know each other better than people that see each other and talk every day. You know about every corner of my existence, and I love you more than life itself. You even know my daughter and the difficulties I have had in being a single parent. You have pictures of us, and you accept me as I am—even knowing my faults. And the picture I have of you only confirms what I know in my heart. You are beautiful inside and out. I am coming to meet you as we have arranged but would like to surprise you now. Will you marry me? I promise to do all I can to make our life together happy and joyous.

Lucy's heart leaped when she read Robert's letter. This was the special man she had fallen in love with and looked forward to meeting with such excitement. She had been divorced for 10 years, never expected to meet anyone with whom she could fall in love, and wasn't really looking. As a busy attorney, her life was full and rich. But Robert had touched a special place. He was everything she was looking for—a caring and sensitive man who had devoted his life to others as a dedicated college professor.

"Yes, my dear man. I will marry you. I'll be at the airport, wearing a red rose and a big smile just for you. Hurry to me," Lucy wrote.

Engaged before even meeting? This is not uncommon in cyberspace. A meeting of the minds can be powerful and compelling. Psychologist Merilyn M. Salomon, interviewed on the popular Jerry Springer daytime talk show, stated that our more conventional avenues for meeting and mating have broken down, enabling the online meeting places to be of far greater importance. "Families or a mediator used to perform this role in our culture," states Dr. Salomon. Of course, sometimes your online friends can feel like a family.

"Computer romances can work, but only if there is complete honesty and no game playing," says Kate, a 46-year-old Ohio nurse who met her husband online six years ago. "You have to be careful not to rush. Time is different in cyberspace. It can move much more quickly. People can become intimate easily as they talk to each other in an anonymous and uninhibited setting." Kate and her husband are happily married today but confess they don't spend much time online anymore...:)

Sometimes people who meet online want a real-life wedding that continues the cyberspace theme. The happy couple sit at computer terminals describing their wedding to online friends connected in their own homes all over the country. These weddings may even take on a spacelike aura, with the bride and groom donning virtual reality headgear or special suits right out of the "Captain Video: Space Cadet" series. What does this mean for the future? Will the wedding chapels in Las Vegas offer new services for those who are computer connected? Will the rules be changed? And will people be legally joined together in ceremonies taking place simultaneously with the bride in Anchorage and the groom in Houston? Only time will tell, but we are headed in that direction.

The following is a press release of just such a real-life wedding that took place as the result of an online love affair. This wedding took place in a judge's chambers with the guests attending—on their computers.

PRESS RELEASE—Virtual Wedding Legally Joins Couple in San Francisco

....

The bride was lovely in white satin; the groom was resplendent in a traditional black tuxedo. And the guests were comfortable in their bathrobes or jeans and sneakers—all many miles apart. It was 8:00 in the morning when the bride said, "I do." The groom quickly responded, "I do, also," and Judge Richard J. Brown beamed at the happy couple. "I pronounce you man and wife!"

This unusual early morning wedding was the result of a computer courtship. Their screen names are FoxEFran and DrDAVE and they met on a computer communication service nearly 13 months earlier. They chatted each morning, fell for each other, talked on the phone, decided to meet—and the rest was wedding album history. It only seemed right to have the wedding online in the early morning "room" where they met, with their computer friends attending—all hooked together via modem.

People the world over are meeting on their computers, falling in love, and deciding to marry. This is the new way for people to meet and mingle. And it is much safer and more fun than the bar scene. It is also more common than most people realize.

CrazyHoss raised his coffee cup high and said, "I would like to make a toast to the happy couple. May all your days be filled with happy computing and speedy downloads." Cups were raised all over the country as everyone added his best wishes. Hugs {{{}}} and smiles :) filled their computer screens. Judge Brown watched his own computer screen as his secretary, Donna Miller, typed a description of the happy couple to everyone. Though there were actually only 4 people in the judge's office, they felt surrounded by warm and loving thoughts.

DrDAVE took FoxEFran into his arms and gave her a huge kiss. They would be repeating their vows later in the day in a real church ceremony for their real-life families and friends, but this was the most meaningful and memorable part of a very special day. Their online friends had watched the romance bloom and felt like they had been a part of it.

"You make a beautiful bride," typed SuzieQ onto her screen in Seattle, wiping a tear. "I'm soooo glad I could witness this special wedding. Here's to many happy years together."

"I want a wedding just like this, " agreed Jane in Florida. "And I want you all to be there with me, too."

•   XXX

Keep an open mind where romance is concerned. Take things slow and easy, but be prepared. Love can find you when you least expect it—even on your computer! If you are looking for a true love in cyberspace, Delilah wishes you all the best of luck and good fortune.

10

Delilah Says . . .

::::::::Pulling chair up to my friendly
computer one more time:::::::

Sharing this information has been wonderfully fun. And we
have only scratched the surface. The technology is in its
infancy, but the baby is growing at a record pace and it's
hard to imagine what the Internet, WWW, and BBSs will be
like even a year from now. In this chapter we will highlight
some important points previously mentioned—in case you
missed them—and add some additional thoughts.

Don't be shy!

When you are a "newbie" it all seems fast and furious
online. People type at terrific speeds and all talk at once.
It's hard to follow the conversation, let alone get a word

in edgewise. Most people feel a bit timid when it comes to posting a response in a newsgroup or typing those first sentences to others, who all seem to know each other and to be so comfortable at their keyboards. But stick your toe in—the water's really fine. And there is room in the virtual hot tub for virtually everyone! As Delilah insists, most people will be friendly and helpful. Just watch to see what the topic, or "thread," is about, then add your thoughts. And don't be shocked if the conversations are explicit.

Many people are not comfortable discussing their sexuality in real life. Husbands and wives are often too embarrassed to discuss their sexual fantasies with each other. But online, in a confidential and anonymous format, mature adults feel free to talk about anything. And some say this freedom is what drives the incredible expansion of membership that online services enjoy. Often, a serious question is posted and the answers are usually caring and thoughtful.

In an ECHO conference, the following was recorded in response to the question "What is the appeal of an online relationship?"

Pat: I think it can satisfy a need two people might have for both intimacy and distance. Some people need a screen for whatever reason. Perhaps they are both married but find an online relationship fulfills a need not being met.

Richard: Are you talking about love or sex?

Pat: Well, sometimes people begin an online relationship with conversation about sex, but one thing leads to another, and if they decide to engage in cybersex and imagine they are really having sex with each other, their relationship can move to a new level. They can find they really care for each other.

Richard: Now are you talking about love?

Pat: I think it's a kind of "love" we don't have a word for.

> It's cyberlove, but it can sometimes grow into real-life love.
>
> Richard: And don't forget there are lots of people with no real sex in their lives—for whatever reason. Computer sex is better than living without...

People love to talk about sex. And why not? They are intensely interested in sex, always have been and always will be. It's part of the human condition. And computer communication is just one more avenue for individuals to express themselves. Is this healthy? Doctors tell us that an active interest in sex increases overall health. And since millions of adults are talking about sex on their computers, some people insist that we are on the verge of a new kind of sexual revolution, one that could lead to less dysfunction in our society, perhaps even fewer divorces. Discussing sex, or trying cybersex, can increase your comfort level with your own sexuality. It can also be educational as you find out what others think about and enjoy doing. Learning about relationships and sex can take many forms, and computers are a tool that allows us to explore our sensuality. We can make simulated love with people all around the world. We can learn about sadomasochism, domination/submission games, or fetishes in a safe environment. Bottom-spanking, hot and sexy pictures, and erotic interactive games can be only a keystroke away.

It's OK to have fun! <grin>

Talking to others on your computer is wonderfully fun. And it's easy to find something to make you smile in cyberspace, something to share with your new friends. On your favorite computer service, click your way onto the Internet, go into the Newsgroups area, and check out the following:

alt.humor.best-of-usenet

alt.humor.puns

bln.humor (in German)

chile.humor (in Spanish)

rec.humor

rec.humor.flame

rec.humor.funny

rec.humor.oracle

You can subscribe to the joke of the day (there are several of these mailing lists) and receive a preselected joke in your mailbox daily. It's a lovely way to start the day, but a word to the wise: Don't forward your funnies to your busy boss, unless you keep 'em brief. A work setting is not the place to play with E-mail. (Remember?) The following is a joke sent out by Scott Anderson in Minnesota to his "Joke of the Day" subscribers.

Don't Let It Happen To You
(As told by the generic Mr. Smith)

When I awoke this morning, I was aware it wasn't an ordinary day. I felt an inner sense that made me want to close my eyes and go back to sleep. Then I remembered it was my birthday, and at my age, who needs another one?

I rose, showered, dressed, and descended the stairs, bracing myself for the usual chorus of "Happy Birthday" from the kids. But there was none. Not even a cheerful "Happy Birthday, Dear" from my wife. Instead of being grateful that so far the world had allowed me to ignore it, I felt even a deeper gloom.

As I entered my office, my lovely blonde secretary greeted me with nothing more than "Good Morning, Mr. Smith." Then at 11:30 it happened. My secretary came in all smiles and said, "It's such a beautiful day, I've decided to take you to a darling little place for lunch to celebrate your birthday."

We arrived, had a few drinks and a wonderful lunch. On the way back to the office, she said "Now we'll stop by my apartment where it is quiet and we will have more privacy." When we arrived, she mixed me a drink and then excused herself to "change into something more comfortable." "Ah," I thought, "life is good after all."

Soon she called out, "Are you ready for my little surprise?" Her bedroom door opened, and there she stood holding a huge birthday cake aglow with candles. There also stood my wife and kids, their eyes aglow with love. And there I stood with nothing on but my socks.

<BG> (Big Grin)

And from the list of 205 "Dumb Blonde" jokes in the rec.humor newsgroup (Delilah has tried soooo hard to be blonde!):

Q. What did the blonde's mum say to her before the blonde's date?
A. If you're not in bed by 12:00, come home.

and...

A dumb blonde died and went to Heaven. When she got to the Pearly Gates, she met Saint Peter, who said, "Before you get to come into Heaven, you have to pass a test." "Oh no!" she said. But Saint Peter said not to worry—he'd make it easy.

"Who was God's son?" said Saint Peter.

The dumb blonde thought for a few minutes and said, "Andy!"

"That's interesting. What made you say that?" said Saint Peter.

Then she started to sing, "Andy walks with me! Andy talks with me! Andy tells me..."

<VBG> (Very Big Grin)

and one Delilah couldn't resist...

Q. Why do blondes have square boobs?
A. Because they forgot to take the tissues out of the box. LOL LOL

<VBSEG> (You figure this out!)

Wait—there's more!

Limerick

There once was a hopeful young suitor
Who met his true love by computer.
He flew to her state
To a terrible fate.
'Cause on the computer, she's cuter!

from the friend of a friend of a friend...:)

153

Let's recap. A sense of humor is important in every area of life, especially in your online life. Expect your family to gather around to see what you are LOL (laughing out loud) about! And don't forget that "we're all akin under the skin." Treat others the way you want to be treated. Larry Green, of NixPix Person-to-Person, says, "If behavior would get you punched, slapped, or ignored at a bar or party, it's inappropriate online also."

Keep an open mind as you explore the world of online communication. Just because a particular point of view doesn't work for you doesn't mean it isn't interesting to someone else. There is true freedom of speech online. And you will have a lot of fun with your new online friends if you let your hair down and shed those old inhibitions. Come on, give free rein to your fantasies.

People in cyberspace are judged by what they think and say, not by their physical appearance. This is a large part of the excitement and promise of online relationships. But don't be fooled. These relationships can reach a deep level of intimacy found rarely in relationships created offline. And most relationships begin by having fun.

Hot chat either appeals or it doesn't. Really gifted writers are few and far between, but when you connect with a master, it can be as captivating as a bestselling erotic novel. If your pseudonym is feminine, you will be pounced on as soon as you log on. Delilah has heard every come-on in the book. If you are a man looking for hot chat, remember that the best approach is a combination of persistence and subtlety. Be patient. Be honest. Be kind. And be romantic. If you are looking for an attentive and willing submissive, the best approach is still a combination of persistence and subtlety. Be forceful. Be demanding. And bring your whip. There is something for EVERYONE in cyberspace.

In an adult room on America Online, the following dialogue was recorded when seven individuals from all over the country decided to have some fun and create their own soap opera. (At least two of these people are grandparents!!) Once more Delilah has changed names and edited a bit...:)

LyndaKay:	Here we go. I'll be the narrator...now ACTION!
Marcy10:	::::::jumping into John's strong arms:::::::::
JohnV123:	:::::::catching Marcy just in time:::::::
LyndaKay:	The passion begins to rool over them in waves of unrelenting LUST
LyndaKay:	rock and rool...LOL
Marcy10:	:::::::lost in John's embrace:::::: Ooooooh, John! {S kiss
Deardee:	What's a rool?
LyndaKay:	That's a sloppy roll...:)
Marcy10:	<BG>
JohnV123:	:::::::embracing Marcy, sweeping her from her feet:::::: My Marcy... {S kiss
Marcy10:	:::::trembling with desire:::::::
BrownBear:	Geez, Marcia, John, what is this room rated??? :)
LyndaKay:	Bear, without vulgarity, it is still PG-13.
AnnieFan:	HI ROOMIES....What's up today in here?
Deardee:	Welcome to our soap opera, Annie. It's just about as real, too.
JohnV123:	{{{{{{{{{{{{hugging Annie in greeting}}}}}}}}}}}}}
Marcy10:	Boy, John, you are soooo fickle...
LyndaKay:	Fickle? Is your pickle fickle, John? LOL
JohnV123:	Who is "soooo fickle"? Certainly not I, while holding Marcy in my arms!
Marcy10:	That's better, John...:)
LyndaKay:	Let's get on with the action...
JohnV123:	Wait just a minute!!! Who said anything about my pickle???????

155

LyndaKay:	Ahhhh, yessss, the thrill of the saga of John and Marcy...
JohnV123:	John's pickle is just fine, LyndaKay!!!!
Marcy10:	Sour and green??
JohnV123:	::::::scooping Marcy up and carrying her off to the loft::::::
LyndaKay:	We just lost our actors...
Deardee:	Really steamy computer sex only takes one person AND the computer...
KRISTOL:	Dee, I disagree. What if we all need two hands to type?
LyndaKay:	What we need are all left-hand words.
AnnieFan:	I'll make a list.
BrownBear:	How about read, seed, was, and tex?
Deardee:	And there's great, treat, card, and tea.
LyndaKay:	Got it! A cad cared to vex free breasts for tests-treated dear Tara...

and so on and so on...
Now for one last joke...:)

An old lady was rocking away the last of her days on her front porch, reflecting on her long life, when all of a sudden a fairy godmother appeared in front of her and informed her that she could have any three wishes she wanted.

"Well," said the old lady, "I guess I would like to be really rich."

ZAP Her rocking chair turned to solid gold.

"And, gee, I guess I wouldn't mind being a young, beautiful princess."

ZAP She turned into a young, beautiful woman.

"Your third wish?" asked the fairy godmother.

Just then the old woman's cat walked across the porch in front of them.

"Can you change him into a handsome prince?" she asked.

ZAP

There before her stood a young man more handsome than she ever could have imagined possible. With a smile that made her knees weak, he sauntered across the porch and whispered in her ear, "Aren't you sorry you had me neutered?"

Make your new friends feel special!

THE GAMEBOX

The Gift—When you find someone you enjoy, show your appreciation for that person's friendship. Send a funny story or joke that you uncovered on the Internet. Make a GIF of your favorite photograph for your new friend. And if you are lucky enough to find love online, send your sweetie a dozen roses @——} ——} —— X 12. Write a beautiful poem or story for that special person.

Send a text file to your online friends. And if you don't want to make your own, you can find them on the Internet in the newsgroup rec.arts.ascii. Learn to cut and paste your favorites.

```
      K\\
       IS\Fr\
      SKISS\om\
      KISSKIS  \Me\            A Chocolate Kiss!
     SKISSKISS
    sKISSKISSKISs
   sSKISSKISSKISSKIs
  sSKISSKISSKISSKISSKI
 SKISSKISSKISSKISSKISSK
 SKISSKISSKISSKISSKISSK
  SKISSKISSKISSKISSKISS
```

```
     love love l          ove love lo
    ve love love love       love love love lov
   e love love love love l  ove love love love love
  love love love love love   love love love love love
 love love love love love l ove love love love love lov
e love love love love love love love love love love love
love love love love love love love love love love love
love love love love love love love love love love love
 love love love love love love love love love love lov
  e love love love love love love love love love lov
  e love love love love love love love love love
   love love love love love love love love love l
   ove love love love love love love love love
    love love love love love love love lov
     e love love love love love love lov
      e love love love love love love
       love love love love love lo
       ve love love love love lo
        ve love love love love          Your Heart!
         love love love
          love love
          love lo
           ve
            l                    jbrennan@alf2.ted.ie
```

Or how about:

```
      .,,,,,,,,,,,
     .,,,,,,,,,,,,,,
    ,,,,,,,,,,,,,,,,,
   ,;;;;;;;;;;;;)));;(((,,;;;,,_
   ,;;;;;;;;;;’    l))))))))))))\
   ;;;;;;/ )’’   ~ /,)))((((((((((\
    /  /   l  (((((((((((((
   /’     _/~’  ‘)l()))))))))         A KISS!
   /’    ` />  o_/)))((((((((
  /    /’`~~(____ /  ()))))))))))
  |  —,     (((((((((
   `  -_____l   ))))))))
    `l   l_.—. \                    —Tua Xiong
```

Or:

```
::::          :::::::     ::::       ::::    :::::::::
::::          :::: ::::   ::::       ::::    :::::::::
::::          ::::  ::::  ::::       ::::    ::::
::::          ::::  ::::  ::::       ::::    :::::::::          LOVE!
::::          ::::  ::::  :::: ::::  ::::
::::          ::::  ::::  ::::::::   ::::
::::::::: :::: ::::    :::::::     :::::::::
::::::::: :::::::        ::::       :::::::::
```

Friendships are very real in cyberspace. In the follow-ing discussion, JudyJudy found out she was very special to her online friends. They really cared about the prob-lem she shared.

JudyJudy:	*I have a serious question this morning, gang. How can you know if your husband is having an affair?*
Raman:	*Lipstick is always a giveaway, Judy.*
Chopstix:	*Have his habits changed? Is he dressing differently, needing time to himself...?*
DeLight:	*Sniff his shirt, Judy, and check for perfume...not yours*
JudyJudy:	*I'm taking notes...*
Raman:	*You COULD have him followed...what are the clues?*
DeLight:	*Sometimes sex will tell the tale—less at home...*
JudyJudy:	*He is never home on time...a change in routine for sure.*
Chopstix:	*Sometimes there is more sex at home—covers the guilt. I know...caught my husband cheating after 22 years.*
DeLight:	*Judy, there are all kinds of arrangements out there. Can you talk about it with him...live with it?*
Raman:	*If you can prove it, kick the bum OUT.*
Chopstix:	*Be careful. Don't over-react. I will E-mail you with more thoughts—based on MY real life experience.*

DeLight: Watch his eyes and the expression on his face when
             you confront him. If he gets indignant or says you
             are crazy, a bad sign.

JudyJudy: I'm going to ask him tonight if he wants to play sex
             games with me on the computer. If he says "Nope," I
             will know...

Perhaps Judy gained some perspective on her problem and was able to work it out. At least she found a sharing, caring group to talk to.

In the following E-mail, you will see just how special Elaine's computer love was to her. She enjoyed their online talktime so much, she was willing to pay for it!

Dear Elaine,

My dearest and sweetest online love...I must tell you that the worst has happened. My wife has found out about my dalliance with you. She is having a fit, and I don't know what to do. I really feel I can't bear to be without our daily times here together, but I have to keep peace at home as well. What to do?

Love and kisses all over, Tom

Dearest Tom, my wild CAT,

Oh NOOOOOO! What can we do? I will truly perish without talking to you here. And what will I do without E-mail from you??? I mean this!

Sunk in Sadness, Elaine

Dear Elaine,

How can I tell you this? My heart is torn into a thousand pieces. My wife put my suitcase by the door and said I could leave or close my account. What else was I to say but "Yes, Dear. I shall close it by week's end." Can you ever forgive me? I will always adore you.

Love forever, Tom

Dear Tom,
Is this all there is?

Your loving E

Dear Elaine,

Well, there is a way we can talk. You know my wife is making me close my online account. BUT since you have 3 names for your account, why not let me sign on using one of your names. All I need to know is the password for that name. Then I can send mail to one of your other names.

Only thing, we can't both be online at the same time. We will have to plan our times to share…

I will write you offline, then sign on and send. I'll only use your account for a few minutes each time. What do you think?

Deeplove, Tom

Deeplove,

Well, what if I opened a second account…then we could both be online at the same time…you could sign onto one account and I could sign onto the other. We could talk to each other as well as send E-mail. Would this work???

Dyingforyou, Elaine

Dearest Dying,

What a brilliant idea. I think it will work and I will send you the money to pay for the time I use. Just let me know my name and password. I love you sooooo much. Let's do this today!!!

YOUR TOM

Dear Tom,

Done!! You are MYOWNTOM and your password is GOTCHA. See you at noon today! Be there!

Smooches, Elaine

Welllll, it seems only fair that since Elaine is covering their online time, she can monitor Tom. And since she knows his password, she can even read his mail!!! LOL LOL

It's worldwide!

People are connecting to the Internet and sharing sexy stuff all over the world. Delilah's world map of the "wired," provided by the Internet Society, ranks technologically sophisticated countries in terms of temperature. Norway, Sweden, and Finland are HOT countries, with 200 people or less for each direct Internet connection. Japan, a MEDIUM country, plans to connect every home to the Internet by the year 2010. And Costa Rica is WARM, the most sophisticated technologically in Central America. Some day the whole world will be online.

In London you can go to Cyberia, a cafe that sells cappuccino along with a half-hour's access to the Internet on one of their computers. (Similar spots have recently opened in New York City and Houston.) In Hong Kong fiber-optic cables are already in place in hundreds of the city's skyscrapers. Political leaders in Europe recognize the importance of being on the "Infobahn." And the United States is the best connected of all, with 32 PCs per 100 people.

Our northern neighbors, the Canadians, have a more open, self-regulating attitude. They have very little policing of their communications services and offer more "freenet" connections (those friendly and cheap networks often funded by a university or local government) than the United States. The Canadians also tend to be more interested in local, rather than world, activities.

France has had the Minitel since the 1980s. It is a small-screen unit with a keyboard that plugs into a normal telephone outlet and has been popular as a connection to both hard- and soft-core pornography. Again, sex rears its head.

The major commercial services are looking carefully at the European marketplace. CompuServe has set up connections in most of Europe's major cities, offering forums and services in French, German, and Dutch. And the *New York Times* reports that a Singapore minister of information predicted that, "The widespread use of English will eventually be contested—the Internet itself will become multicultural." Perhaps Unicode, with far more character sets, will replace ASCII code, commonly used now.

It is interesting to note that in several countries with advanced technology and active use of the Internet, there is little censorship of anything, and the status of women in these countries is very high. In his book *Sex and Reason,* Richard A. Posner points out that in Sweden and Denmark women enjoy a very liberated and high status, yet pornography is widely circulated. And both men and women are active users of the Internet in these countries.

Computer communication is connecting our whole world in a new way. Try it. Log on and look for the international connections. Share a new idea. Share a joke. Enjoy these incredible opportunities. They are everywhere.

Where do we go from here?

We are not very good at predicting the future. No one could imagine how Johannes Gutenberg's invention of the printing press would shape lives, even history. But it seems everyone is trying to predict where our computers are taking us. Nicholas Wade, of the *New York Times,* insists that, "Technology does change society, but on a time scale of decades, not years." It has taken 20 years for the VCR to find a place in American homes. And James Coates, who writes about computers for the *Chicago Tribune,* says, "Computers will soon become so much a part of our lives, we won't even know they are there." In many ways, this has already happened.

Virtual reality is here and developing new uses every day. Surgeons are testing it for virtual operations, architects are using it to develop new building ideas, and it is being used by young people in the classroom and in the game parlor. Designers, the military, and entertainment executives are smacking their collective lips as they contemplate the future possibilities, but because this chapter is primarily concerned with sex and computer communication, let's take a look at teledildonics (the use of electronic communication in conjunction with sexual artifacts). Some call this virtual, or digital, sex.

Imagine putting on special "space suits" and plugging into a device that transports you and your partner into another medium, where you feel the sensation on your fingertips of touching silky hair or warm skin and kissing soft lips. Of course, each person would be alone at his or her own computer terminal, maybe halfway around the world from each other. Kathy Keeton, of General Media International, calls this a "neuromimetic sexual experience," where your nerves translate sensations into electronic pulses. You could have an intensely sexual adventure—better than today's cybersex—without any real contact. Would you like to take a trip like this? Lots of movie directors believe you would. Remember *Total Recall* and *Lawnmower Man?* They were just the beginning.

Teledildonics seems to be at the top of the list in any discussion about the future of computer communication. In fact, so much has been said about this in the media that many believe it is available. In actuality, this special equipment is still in the experimental stages. However, it will no doubt be available in the near future since technology and sex continue to search for common ground. "I sure hope I live long enough for this!" says HappyJack, in an online discussion about the future of teledildonics.

Harvey P. Newquist III writes in *AI Expert* that data gloves and vision helmets will be a part of it. You may crawl into "some form of tight-fitting bodysuit with force feedback or pulse generators located in specific areas of the suit." Are you able to picture this? Use your imagination. You might enjoy assuming the body of the opposite sex, or maybe even both sexes at once. Or perhaps you'd like to see what it's like to make love as a Robomaster, tying a gorgeous wench to your computer table. Be an alien or a snake or even create new types of sexual sensation. If you have a foot fetish, you could give feet new hot spots. Instead of using a vibrator, you could be a vibrator. Will two "thingees" be better than one? Will four "thingees" be better than two? "With the participants outfitted in similar snug-fitting garb and sharing the same telecom link, they can reach out, touch each other, and do whatever it is they feel like doing," says Newquist. Is this sex? We'll explore that question when we've had the opportunity to play in these special bodysuits! We may need to redefine a few things. LOL

Dear readers—it has been great fun, but now we are nearing the end of our journey through cyberspace. The appendices that follow will give you a general overview of the Internet—the newsgroups and World Wide Web— as well as some favorite spots to visit.

::::::::smiling encouragement:::::::

Appendix A

Can You Make It Simple?

Q. As a "newbie" I am very confused. Can you explain the Internet in simple terms? What are newsgroups? And what is the World Wide Web?

Kayla in IL

A. A big question! And, remember, this is a guide to what to say online, not a hands-on instruction manual on how to navigate the Internet. There are plenty of fine books to help you do that, like the net.guides published by Random House. But let's give it a try. Here's a basic and general summary.

What's the Internet?

The Internet is the mother of all networks. The U.S. Department of Defense 20-odd years ago began an experimental computer network that they hoped could withstand any nuclear attack. It's made up of local area networks, citywide metropolitan area networks, and huge wide-area networks connecting computer organizations all over the world. It uses telephone lines, satellites, microwave links, and fiber-optic links. Trying to map it is like trying to count the stars. Tracy LaQuey calls it a "cloud." And unlike the major online services, the Internet is not primarily geared toward a user-friendly atmosphere. But its worldwide communication capabilities and entrance to academic and government research make it enormously powerful. It provides access to numerous resources—over 20,000 newsgroups (special interest forums) and millions of data files and software programs—by seamlessly connecting hundreds of thousands of computers and tens of millions of people all over the globe. No one owns or controls it, and the vast majority of Internet features are free. Your charges come with the method you choose to access all this—your BBS or commercial service.

The Internet can be confusing at first, but its content, resources, and services are really quite straightforward. The most useful include the following: *E-mail, newsgroups,* and the *World Wide Web (WWW).* Now, pretend you are in Delilah's Internet 101 class, and we will make these as simple as possible.

If you have gotten this far, you have a good understanding of E-mail, that wonderful electronic way of sending messages to any other Internet user in the world. E-mail is what the majority of people use the most on the Net. And you know that there are programs that allow you to attach a file to your E-mail, which might contain a graphic, formatted document, sound file, etc. E-mail has changed the lives of people who use computers. Onliners take their mail very seriously, as you will see in the following conversation. This was recorded on America Online one early morning when the mail function wasn't quite up to par.

KatyDid: What on earth is wrong with my mail this morning?

Jeannie: Don't have a pissy attitude, Katy. It works INTERMIT-TENTLY—just to make life interesting…:)

Chris: Hi folks…what's up with the mail?

KatyDid: How come yours works and mine doesn't, Jeannie?

Randyman: Does anyone know how long the mail will be down?

Jeannie:	Beats me...I just checked it...really I did!!
SallyNY:	HELP—NO MAIL...I am having a heart attack...
Jeannie:	Perhaps I have mail 'cause I live in VA...home of AOL
SallyNY:	I have to get to my mail, read it, then delete it before my husband gets home!!!
Nancy:	Good Sally...that's really funny!
Chris:	Looks to me like cyber-romance has been given a serious setback here.
SallyNY:	If my husband logs on and sees my mail, my online lovers will be explosed!!!
SallyNY:	I mean exposed. I'm so upset, I can't even type!
Chris:	Explosed? Sounds painful, Sally...<grin>
Randyman:	Maybe we could call the US Govt. and they could help us here with our mail.
Chris:	You mean fall back on the US Postal Service now? I think NOT...
SallyNY:	My mail is red HOT. People would pay to read my mail. I do!!!
Jeannie:	Just change your password, Sally. Then your husband can't read your mail.
SallyNY:	That would make him really suspicious, Jeannie.
Randyman:	Everyone online is complaining about the mail this morning!
SallyNY:	::::::dialing Vienna, VA:::::: ring, ring, ring, ring
SallyNY:	Hello, Steve? Where the hell is my mail??????
KatyDid:	Don't hold back, Sally! Let your feelings out. LOL LOL (laughing out loud)
Brad101:	Morning, roomies. {{{{{{{hugs to all}}}}}}}
SallyNY:	:::::draping the computer in black crepe:::::::
Nancy:	My husband doesn't care what mail I get.
Chris:	Well—makes me no nevermind. I get all my mail at CompuServe anyway.

Randyman: Gosh, Sally...maybe you should have your mail sent
to me...:)

Brad101: Is all the mail broken?

And so on and so on...

What are Newsgroups?

Similar to the forums and message boards on commercial
online services, Internet newsgroups are interactive bulletin boards where you can read what others have posted, then add something or tack up your own message.
Every newsgroup is different, and your online service or
BBS will provide you with a list of the most common.
There are new newsgroups every day, but you can stay
current by checking magazines and newspapers that
keep up with such things. Then, just click your way into
the Internet Newsgroup section of your service and type
in the newsgroup address. Sounds easy, until you consider that there are 20,000 of them, as mentioned, and we
may have more than half a million by the turn of the cen-
tury. One good online resource for newsgroup newcom-
ers is David Lawrence's newsgroup list, which gives you
thousands of newsgroup names and often, a witty one-
line description. To get to this list, check out this
address: news.lists.

Newsgroups are more discussion than news, about
anything and everything, and can be from anywhere in
the world. They are frivolous or serious, funny or outrageous. They are addictive. They are a free, uncensored
exchange of ideas, opinions, comments, and anything
goes. You will need a newsgroup newsreader to access
these messages, which your online service or BBS will
provide. When you find a newsgroup you enjoy, you may
be able to get on a mailing list and automatically get the

new posts in your E-mail mailbox daily.

Newsgroups (and the Web) have addresses that are much different from E-mail addresses. These addresses go from the general to the specific as you read from left to right. And there are seven "official" categories of newsgroups as well as a bunch of "alternative" ones. The big seven are: comp (computer stuff), news (about newsgroups), rec (recreation), sci (science), soc (social issues), talk (debate), and misc (everything else). The most used alternative categories include: alt (bizarre things), bit (mailing lists), biz (business), and clari (commercial news). A newsgroup address for serious information might be sci.space.news. And a more frivolous newsgroup might be found at alt.beer.

If you are looking for the sexy stuff and your taste tends toward the alternative, some interesting reading can be found in alt.sex or alt.personals.spanking.punishment, alt.sex.strip-clubs, and even alt.sex.fetish.fashion. These are areas that seem to stimulate heated discussions, even discussions on freedom of speech. The large commercial services like CompuServe, America Online, and Prodigy forbid the posting of sexually explicit material, but once you are out on the Internet, there are no police. Many people are shocked to read, see, or hear things that are intensely pornographic. But more than half the Internet users are outside the legal jurisdiction of the United States, so, on the Internet, anything goes!

What's the World Wide Web (WWW)?

Think of this as a sort of guide, superimposed over the Internet. Paul Bonnington, the publisher of *Internet* magazine, has called the World Wide Web the "Fourth Media"—after print, radio, and television—as a mass-market means of communication. A common error is to consider the Web and the Internet to be synonymous. Actually, the Web is a collection of standards and protocols, or tools, used to access the information available on the Internet. Because of its graphical interface—the wonderful pictures that lead you from place to place—the Web makes the Internet easy to "surf," or explore.

Using your BBS or online service Web browser, you can click your way onto the Web and view "pages" ("webtalk" for screens filled with text and graphics). There are more than 250,000 Web pages created by companies, magazines, newspapers, and individuals. Using a special software program and some study, anyone can create a page. Having your own Web page is like having an online business card. And when you click your mouse on highlighted words, also called "links," on these Web pages, you are transported to other related pages with additional information, which might include snippets of movies or songs and colorful pictures or graphics. These links are called *hypertext*. HTTP means Hypertext Transfer Protocol but is really just a webway of moving around. Sound like fun? Pick up some books to help you. Hours fly by as you "surf the Net."

Another Web abbreviation you see a lot is URL, meaning Uniform Resource Locator, and a URL is an address. It specifies the three pieces of information necessary to move you through cyberspace: protocol to be used, server and port to connect, and file path to retrieve. A good example of an award-winning World Wide Web address, or URL, is http://www-swiss.ai.mit.edu/samantha/travels-with-samantha.html.

This wonderful site with many graphics is based on the online only book *Travels with Samantha*, by Philip Greenspun. He is at M.I.T. in Cambridge, MA, and you will quickly see why this site is so popular.

Notice the initials "html" on the end of most WWW addresses. This is the last WWW abbreviation you should recognize. It means Hypertext Markup Language, and "html" is a format for tagging text in a document so it can be translated for any system. Sometimes you will see that the last "l" is omitted.

THE GAMEBOX

Delilah's Home Page—Pay a visit to Delilah at her own home page. Her URL, or address, is http://www.delilah.com/askme. Do you have a question for Delilah? Send your question to: AskDelilah@aol.com.

Check her home page for answers, and if she answers YOUR question on her home page, give yourself five points!

Using what you have learned

In this section, we will introduce you to some concepts and terms that you might want to explore in some detail. Yep, this is a bit of a detour.

Using FTP, or File Transfer Protocol, you can download files of software, text, and graphics from companies, universities, libraries, museums—all on the Internet. Remember to get permission to use ALL copyrighted materials! FTP is a major utility, and although a thorough discussion of its mechanics is beyond the scope of this book, you should explore the richness available. The quantity of information is impossible to measure. Anything and everything is available. How about checking out the budget of the U.S. government? Or the Russian telephone directory? :) And the wonder of FTP is that it makes it possible to transfer materials no matter what kind of machine you are using or what kind of machine is holding the file you want.

If you don't know what you want and just want to

browse, you will want to use a Gopher server (the original Gopher was named after the University of Minnesota mascot). Gopher servers present Internet data in a menu format, and the tool that searches the Gopher servers is Veronica. As you might guess, there is even a Jughead search tool. Perhaps these comic-strip names were intended to put a light touch on something that can be incredibly complex and daunting, even for computer programmers, and certainly a WAIS (another search tool, pronounced "ways") beyond this book! So rush to your bookstores or sign up for some classes. All good things take some time and practice.

The following URL has a great online directory of Web sites to visit: http://www.yahoo.com.

Anything else?

Of course! As you explore this wonderful new world, you will want to check out CD-ROM. This means Compact Disk-Read Only Memory. It is a read-only optical storage drive that uses compact disks. These CDs are similar to regular audio disks except they can store graphics and video. They store many times more pictures—200 or so—than a floppy disk. While not a necessity to online communication, if you want to get into adult videos or high-resolution graphics collections you will need to explore CD-ROM. To view CD-ROM disks, you need a CD-ROM drive that is compatible with your Mac or PC. Since these video products require large amounts of RAM operating system memory and high speed, you will need at least a 486 PC. Many new computers come with a CD-ROM drive already installed. If you have a choice, go for it. Buy the most you can afford right in the beginning. Welcome to cyberspace.

You can have a complete encyclopedia, dictionary,

thesaurus, book of quotations, atlas, and almanac, complete with word pronunciations and video clips, all on one CD-ROM disk. Or buy books bundled together, 10 to a disk. Look at art from all over the world or learn a new sport from a master. Even Betty Crocker has an electronic cookbook, with 1,500 recipes.

Computer video enables you to play interactive games, like *Myst* and *Gadget*. In fact, games abound, and moving images and animations are lots of fun. As you might expect, adult games are very popular. *Virtual Valerie* may be the best-selling CD-ROM ever, with about 25,000 sales a year for four years running. It's the best-selling adult title, capturing about 25% of the entire market. In this game Valerie draws you into her apartment house where you can talk to her, look at her artwork, even use her bathroom, or peek into her purse. The whole point is to interact with Val, and if you say the right things, she will let you undress her...and more.

Check out MUDs. They are "multi-user dimension" programs, and there are thousands running on the Internet. They are pure fantasy environments. When you enter a MUD, you adopt a persona, become a conquering hero or a bear or even a chocolate cake. Then you chat with other characters, solve puzzles, play games, etc. MUDs began with a small cult following but have become very popular for either adventure or social interaction.

And last, but not least, check out the freenets that have sprung up all over the place—even in Wellington, New Zealand, and Victoria, B.C. They are some of the friendliest and cheapest communities on the Internet. These networks are usually funded by a local university, local government, or the private sector. Some are totally free, and some charge small access fees. On a freenet, you can be either a visitor or a registered user with an E-mail address. You can search for information or chat with your neighbor. Perhaps these free community networks will someday connect people in towns and cities worldwide.

We hope this overview helps. Jump in. You will love it. Just remember to keep a very open mind as you play online. You now understand that the Internet is global, and no matter what the future holds, it is changing communication for all time.

Now, ya'll play nice! <VBG>

::::::::*waving good-bye and shutting off the 'puter*::::::::

Appendix B

Delilah's Picks — BBSs

Q. What are your favorite BBS services?

Geoff in CO

A. Here are my picks as of this writing! Check out the computer magazines, like BBS magazine—for sooooo many more.

1. *Aline, Newcom LINK* (Club Aline and Virtual NY)—a French BBS with international membership and tied to *New York* magazine (spicy chat with a French flavor—information about restaurants and theater in NYC—fairly expensive). Modem No. (212) 826-3894.

2. *The Data Highway*—from Ft. Lauderdale, Florida, and mostly for professionals and entrepreneurs with multiplayer games, chat, and conferences about "real" issues. It is a place to meet, network, and play. Inexpensive. Modem No. (305) 797-9841.

3. *ECHO*—in NYC is very user-friendly to women— "cerebral" chat with creative and accomplished people—many conference centers. Moderate. Modem No. (212) 989-8411.

4. *The English Palace*—in Hazlet, New Jersey, is a

friendly place to meet for those into B&D and
S&M, then join for offline social activities such as
dinners, picnics, etc. and Delilah wonders about
real-life whip cracking?? (chat, files, forums)
Moderate. Modem No. (908) 739-0142.

5. *Hall of Records*—in Hendersonville, North Carolina,
is a friendly place to discuss genealogical information. It also offers a catalog with computers and
equipment for sale (networking, newsgroups, and
files). Inexpensive. Modem No. (704) 692-0300.

6. *Odyssey*—in California offers everything—GIFs,
games, travel reservations, and lotsa spicy forums.
This board specializes in matchmaking. Moderate.
Modem No. (818) 358-6968.

7. *Texas Talk*—in Richardson, Texas, is for those
who like down-home, friendly chat. It sponsors
social activities and is a good place to meet a real
cowboy. Inexpensive. (214) 680-4303.

8. *The Transom*—in New York is geared to those who
want to share intelligent conversation and
exchange ideas about important issues of the day.
Moderate. Call for software. (212) 274-0444.

9. *The WELL*—from Sausalito, California, is a good
place to meet new people and chat about new
things. (Conferences about spirituality, music, sexuality.) Fairly expensive. Phone (415) 332-4335.

10. *Windup*—in New York is like an exclusive club for
adults to talk about anything. Membership is kept
to about 300 and they must be at least 21 years
old. (GIF library.) Moderate. Modem No. (718) 428-
6736.

Appendix C

Delilah's Picks — Internet Newsgroups

Q. What are your favorite Internet newsgroups?

ChiTownTim

A. Here they are.

1. alt.alien.visitors (messages about things spacy)

2. alt.backrubs FAQ (great advice here)

3. alt.bbs.majorbbs (messages about bulletin board services)

4. alt.beer (discuss all kinds of beer, including home recipes)

5. alt.fan.letterman.top-ten (Letterman's top ten lists)

6. alt.lifestyle.barefoot (lists upcoming barefoot events and vacations)

7. alt.personals (200 personals posted a day!)

8. alt.romance FAQ (just romance)

9. alt.sex.exhibitionism (interested in driving naked?)

10. alt.sex.fetish (some you have never heard of!)

11. alt.sex.first-time (some interesting first-time stories)

12. alt.sex.playboy (talk with other fans of *Playboy* magazine)

13. alt.sex.stories (wild stories, many worth only a brief scan)

14. alt.sex.telephone (talk about phone sex)

15. alt.sports (isn't everyone into sports?)

16. alt.tasteless.jokes (jokes to share)

17. misc.health.alternative (broad discussions of health issues, products, and techniques)

18. rec.arts.erotica (moderated newsgroup for the best of erotica)

19. rec.arts.movies.reviews (movie reviews)

20. rec.humor (funny stuff)

Appendix D

Delilah's Picks —
World Wide Web Sites

Q. What are you favorite Web pages to visit?

Henry in CT

A. As of today, these work for me. But remember, they come and go...and move!

1. http://anther.learning.cs.cmu.edu/priest.html (The Digital Priest is waiting here at the Confession Booth.)

2. http://meta.stanford.edu/quotes.html (amazing quotes)

3. http://metaverse.com/vibe/ (Adam Curry's site for info on contemporary music)

4. http://postcards.www.media.mit.edu/Postcards (Send a postcard to your sweetheart!)

5. http://sashimi.wwa.com:1111 (Virtual Meetmarket with *lots* of men looking for women)

6. http://ucsub.colorado.edu/~kritzber/new/babes.html (Beauty pageant for MEN)

7. http:www.artnet.org/iamfree (Internet Arts

Museum with photos, literature, music, etc.)

8. http://www.awa.com (Downtown anywhere—shopping!)

9. http://www.galcit.caltech.edu/~ta/rmill.html (Rumor mill with strange stuff and links to other strange stuff)

10. http://www.infi.net/cool.html (Cool sites of the day links)

11. http://www.ird.net/diningout.html (Directory of restaurant sites on the Net)

12. http://www.neosoft.com/citylink (links to all the states and all sorts of info)

13. http://www.onramp.net/imagemaker (catalog for dog lovers with doggie-embossed items)

14. http://www.paranoia.com/drugs (hard facts about drugs)

15. http://www.pcgifts.ibm.com (PC Gifts and Flowers will send real gifts and flowers to your sweetheart)

16. http://www.playboy.com (Doesn't everyone read *Playboy?*)

17. http://www.randomhouse.com/ (Check out the newest books!!!)

18. http://www.surgery.com/body/topics/body.html (Body Space—plastic surgery methods)

19. http://www-swiss.ai.mit.edu/samantha/travels-with-samantha.html (about the online book *Travels with Samantha*)

20. http://www.warhol.org/warhol (works of Andy Warhol)

Appendix E

Internet Addresses

World Wide Web Sites *Page*
(see also Appendix D)

Glossary

America Online Large online service based in Vienna, VA, specializing in chat or discussion forums

bash A real-life get-together of online friends

baud rate Measure of speed (signal changes) at which information is transferred

BBS Computer bulletin board service, often including discussion groups, live chat conferences, E-mail, etc.

bit A single binary number

boot To turn the computer system on, or a two-step dance at the Sundance Saloon :)

bps Bits per second or the number of bits that can be transferred in one second

browser A World Wide Web search tool

byte A unit of eight bits in a computer memory

CD-ROM Compact Disk-Read Only Memory—a read-only optical storage technology that uses compact disks

compatibility Ability of hardware and software to work together

CompuServe One of the biggest online services, based in Columbus, OH

conference Message base devoted to discussion of a specific topic

crash Complete failure of a computer system :(

cursor Small flashing guide to show you where the characters you type will appear on your computer screen

cybersex Also called Csex or compusex, simulated sex through typed description on computers—incredible, funny, kinky, and fantastic

cyberspace The virtual world of online communication, a space behind your screen

Delphi An online service based in Cambridge, MA

digital Having to do with numbers, electronic code used by computers

disk Hard disk is hidden inside the computer and used to store large amounts of data

diskette Small disk called a floppy disk for storing smaller amounts of computer information (two sizes and two densities)

disk crash May require replacement of disk

DOS Disk Operating System—basic system software that controls the PC

download (n) A file of information retrieved from another computer system; (v) the act of retrieving information from another computer system

echo Message base that is echoed to other members regionally, nationally, or even globally

E-mail Electronic messages sent from one bulletin board to another

emoticons Computer symbols used to express emotion :)

encrypt To hide in code

FAQ Frequently asked question

FAX Facsimile transmission or sending an image over a phone line to be reproduced by a distant fax machine

file download To transmit a file from another computer system into your own

file upload To transmit a file from your computer system to another

flames Words used to provoke or embarrass someone

flame-thrower One who uses flames

flame war Several flame users in a heated discussion

freenet Public-access bulletin board, usually set up, maintained, and operated on a nonprofit basis

FTP File Transfer Protocol—tool used in downloading files on the Net

Genie Online service based in Rockville, MD

GIF Graphic Interchange Format—universal viewing format that has become the standard graphics format for PCs

gig One thousand twenty-four megabytes

Gopher Access software used to find information by name on the Internet, like an index

hacker A Dedicated computer programmer, hacking away at problem solving

hacker B Online intruder attempting unauthorized entry into a computer system, hacking away at someone's password

hot chat Compusex or online sexual conversation

HTML Hypertext Markup Language—text language that allows links to other addresses on the Internet

HTTP Hypertext Transfer Protocol—primary tool used to retrieve information on the World Wide Web

IM Instant message

Internet A network of networks with thousands of subnetworks, all sharing the same addressing scheme (Delilah100@aol.com)

IRC Internet Relay Chat—a live chatting service on the Internet with thousands of channels all over the world

Jughead Tool used to search a specific site on the Internet

kilobyte One thousand bytes

log To establish a connection gaining access to a computer system or to record a conference to a file

lurker A digital voyeur, one who watches but doesn't participate (also called a "ghost")

Mac Macintosh computer developed by Apple, favored by graphic artists

macro A simple program that plays back a series of keystrokes

megabyte One thousand twenty-four kilobytes

Microsoft Network (MSN) An online service included with Microsoft's Windows 95 program.

modem Interface device between a computer and a phone line

moderator A volunteer or sysop in a particular conference who settles quarrels and keeps the discussion on track

mouse A small mouse-shaped device that lets you move the cursor on your computer screen

mouse pad Where the mouse lives, or a small sponge or fiber pad allowing one to move the rolling ball beneath the mouse

MUD Multi-User Dimension—allows for role-playing games in fantasy environments

Net Short for Internet

netiquette Online etiquette

newbie One new to online communication

newsgroups Discussion groups on the Internet for posting messages about a topic, or "thread"

offline Not connected to a bulletin board

online When a computer system is connected via modem to a bulletin board communication system

PC Personal Computer, or microcomputer by IBM based on the Intel chip set that can run the software written for the DOS operating system

Pentium Computer chip #80586 that allows your computer to work faassst

posting A message left on a bulletin board newsgroup

Prodigy Large commercial service co-owned by IBM and Sears Roebuck & Co.

RAM Random Access Memory—a computer's electronic memory as opposed to the magnetic storage of a disk

ROM Read Only Memory

scanner Device like a small copying machine to create a computer-saved file

shareware Copyrighted computer program made available on a trial basis

software The instructions a computer follows to perform any task

software crash Usually correctable by rebooting

soundboard Hardware facilitating audio capability

surf Also "cruising" or checking out online areas of interest

sysop System operator/controller of a bulletin board service

teledildonics The use of sexual artifacts in simulated sex

terminal A keyboard and monitor without a central processor or memory capacity

thread Messages in a conference that address the same theme

TOS Terms Of Service—America Online

tos'd Removed from America Online for violating their TOS

URL Uniform Resource Locator—Internet address

USENET Discussion groups on the Internet

Veronica Searches all sites by name on the Internet for specific information

virtual In effect, though not in name, or something that takes place only in cyberspace

virtual reality A simulation of real life

WAIS Wide Area Information Service—a tool that searches file contents on the Internet

windows A windows-based operating system for the PC from Microsoft

World Wide Web (WWW) A kind of guide superimposed on the Internet with "pages" of information and links to other "pages"

zines Online magazine Web sites

References

Much has been written about computer online communication. The subject is explored in magazines and newspapers daily. To keep up-to-date, browse your newsstands and bookstores often. Magazines such as *BBS, Internet World, Online Access,* and *Wired* are worth reading regularly. The following sources have been invaluable to this project:

Baker, Nicholson. *VOX.* New York: Vintage Contemporaries, 1992.

Beard, Steve. "The Future is Fe/male." *i-D,* pp. 84–87, January 1995.

Bennahum, David. "Our Brilliant Careers." *NetGuide,* pp. 49–56, April 1995.

Bowden, Bruce. "Online Seductions." *Penthouse Forum,* pp. 42–46, September 1992.

Browne, Bob. "BBS Notebook." *BBS,* pp. 40–41, February 1995.

Castro, Janice. "Just Click to Buy." *Time,* pp. 74–75, Spring 1995.

Chesebro, James W., and Bonsall, Donald G. *Computer-Mediated Communication.* Alabama: The University of Alabama Press, 1989.

Coates, James. "Binary Beat." *Chicago Tribune,* February 12, 1995.

Coates, James. "Smaller Bulletin Boards Trampling the Giants." *Chicago Tribune,* November 4, 1994.

Coates, James. "Cyperspace." Chicago Tribune, Friday, Sect. 7, July 15, 1994.

Coates, James. "Making Sense of the Online Universe." *Chicago Tribune,* February 18, 1994.

Coates, James. "If You Can't Beat 'Em, Modem." *Chicago Tribune Magazine,* pp. 10–15, February 13, 1994, Sect. 10.

Coates, James. "From On-Line Hangout to Data Superhighway." *Chicago Tribune,* January 16, 1994.

Computer Life magazine staff. "How Do You Know When You're Hooked." *Computer Life,* p. 31, March 1995, copyright © 1995 Ziff-

Davis Publishing Company L.P.

Coupland, Douglas. *microserfs*. New York: Harper Collins, 1995.

Dickerson, John. "Never Too Old." *Time,* p. 41, Spring 1995.

Ellsworth, Jill. "Boom Town." *Internet World,* pp. 32–35, June 1995.

Elmer-DeWitt, Philip. "Welcome to Cyberspace." *Time,* pp. 4–11, Spring 1995.

Flynn, Laurie. "Gauging an Audience in Cyberspace." *New York Times,* May 29, 1995.

Gehl, John. "Edupage." 8/8/95.

Gehl, John. "TechWatch." *Educom Review,* pp. 5–6, May/June 1995.

Glossbrenner, Alfred. "Internet 101—How to Survive in Cyberspace." *Computer Currents,* Aug. 1995, Chicago edition.

Godin, Seth. *Smiley Dictionary.* Berkeley, CA: Peachpit Press, 1993.

Godwin, Mike. "Cops on the I-Way." *Time,* pp. 62–64, Spring 1995.

Godwin, Mike. "Running Scared." *Internet World,* pp. 96–98. April 1995.

Gottesman, Andrew. "E-Mail Becoming Noteworthy." *Chicago Tribune,* February 28, 1994.

Hays, Laurie. "Personal Effects." *Wall Street Journal,* November 15, 1993.

Illingworth, Montieth. "Looking for Mr. Goodbyte." *MiraBella,* pp. 108–117, December 1994.

Jackson, James O. "It's a Wired, Wired World." *Time,* pp. 80–82, Spring 1995.

Jacobson, Linda. *Cyber Arts.* San Francisco, CA: Miller-Freeman, 1992.

Kantor, Andrew. "Ain't it the Truth." *Internet World,* pp. 16–20, October 1995.

Katz, Jon. "The Tales They Tell in Cyberspace." *New York Times,* January 23, 1994.

Keegan, Paul. "The Digerati!" *New York Times Magazine,* May 21, 1995, Section 6.

Keizer, Gregg. "The Internet Made Easy." *Computer Life*, March 1995.

Kendrick, Walter. *The Secret Museum: Pornography in Modern Culture.* New York: Viking Press, 1987.

Kukla, Brenda. "10 Popular Newsgroups." *Online Access,* pp. 30–31,

April 1995.

Lamb, Linda, and Peek, Jerry. *Using email Effectively.* Sebastopol, CA: O'Reilly & Associates, 1995.

LaQuey, Tracy. *The Internet Companion.* Reading, MA: Addison-Wesley, 1993.

Laws, Rita. "All About Online Chat." *Online Access,* pp. 62–66, April 1995.

Lewis, Peter H. "An Atlas of Information Services." *New York Times,* November 1, 1994.

Lewis, Peter H. "A Cyberspace Atlas: America Online." *New York Times,* November 15, 1994.

Lewis, Peter H. "Technology." *New York Times,* May 29, 1995.

Lewis, Peter H. "Technology on the Net." *New York Times,* May 29, 1995.

Lichtenberg, James. "Of Steeds and Stalking Horses." *Educom Review,* pp. 40–43, May/June 1995.

Lichty, Tom. *The Official America Online Tour Guide.* Chapel Hill, NC: Ventana Press, 1993.

Madigan, Charles. "Going with the Flow." *Chicago Tribune Magazine,* May 2, 1993.

Mandell, Tom. "Confessions of a Cyberholic." *Time,* p. 57, Spring 1995.

Mavrides, Melanie. "Youth's Parody on the Internet." *New York Times,* May 28, 1995.

Mossberg, Walter. "Personal Technology." *Wall Street Journal,* April 20, 1995.

Negroponte, Nicholas. *Being Digital.* New York: Alfred A. Knopf, 1995.

Newquist, Harvey P. "Reach Out and Touch Someone." *AI Expert,* August 1993.

Pitt-Kethley, Fiona. *The Literary Companion to Sex.* New York: Random House, 1994.

Posner, Richard A. *Sex and Reason.* Cambridge, MA: Harvard University Press, 1994.

Resnick, Rosalind. *Exploring the World of Online Services.* Alameda, CA: SYBEX, 1993.

Rheingold, Howard. *Virtual Community.* Reading, MA: Addison-Wesley, 1993.

Richard, Eric. "Anatomy of the World-Wide Web." *Internet World*, pp. 28–30. April 1995.

Robinson, Phillip, and Tomosaitis, Nancy. *The Joy of CYBERSEX.* New York: Brady Publishing, 1993.

Rothfeder, Jeff. "To Have and To Hold." *NetGuide,* pp. 76–79, April 1995.

Smolowe, Jill. "Intimate Strangers." *Time,* pp. 20–24, Spring 1995.

Steele, Shari. "Age and Innocence." *BBS,* pp. 28–29, February 1995.

Tomosaitis, Nancy. *net.talk.* Emeryville, CA.: Ziff-Davis, 1994.

VanBakel, Roger. "Mind over Matter." *Wired,* pp. 80–87, April 1995.

Van Der Leun, Gerard. "Twilight Zone of the Id." *Time,* pp. 36–37, Spring 1995.

Wade, Nicholas. "Method and Madness." *New York Times Magazine,* p. 14, January 16, 1994.

Washburn, Bill. "Who's Making Money on the Net?" *Internet World,* pp. 30–31, June 1995.

Wells, Carol. *Right-Brain Sex.* New York: AVON Books, 1991.

Welz, Gary. "New Deals." *Internet World,* pp. 36–42, June 1995.

Wiggins, Richard. "Webolution." *Internet World,* pp. 32–38. April 1995.

Winspear, Violet. *Satan Took a Bride.* New York: Harlequin Books Mills and Boon Ltd., 1975.

Wood, Lamont. *Get On-Line!* New York: John Wiley & Sons, 1993.

Zilbergeld, Bernie. *The New Male Sexuality.* New York: Bantam, 1992.

Coffee Mug

Be the first to have your very own LOL® coffee mug, the perfect companion to Delilah's books. These mugs are jet black with white LOL® lettering and are dishwasher and microwave safe.

To order your LOL® mug, fill out the order form below and mail with payment of $10.00 for each mug to:

Delilah
P.O. Box 1402
Highland Park, IL 60035

Please send LOL® Coffee Mug(s)

Name: _____

Address: _____

_____

No. of mugs wanted:_____

Amt. enclosed:_____